No Time to Chat

Slocum had been cautious leaving the Hangman's Noose Saloon but thought the gambler was on the run. He didn't expect the attack that came at him when he rounded the corner.

A heavy log swinging for his face caused him to duck but the wood only grazed the top of his head and staggered him.

"Who're you?" Slocum called, stumbling back as he recovered his senses. He had thought Ferguson was the club wielder who had attacked him but this man was hard of face and roughly dressed. Behind him came up a second man, equally tough-looking.

Slocum found talking wasn't what the two men had in mind. They both rushed him. He swung and hit one, knocking him aside. But Slocum was off-balance and fell against the building, leaving him wide open for the second man's attack. Strong arms circled his waist. The two men fell to the ground—neither was able to land a solid punch.

Finally, twisting around, Slocum got to his hands and knees. As the man approached him, Sloucm kicked out like a mule. His foot landed smack in the middle of the man's belly. But the first man surged at Slocum again, this time brandishing a knife with a long, wickedly shining blade.

"I'm gonna kill you for this, Slocum."

"You had your chance," Slocum said coldly. He cocked his six-gun again but before he could aim it he heard another, more ominous sound—the noise a double-barreled shotgun makes when both hammers are pulled back.

JAKE LOGAN

SLOCUM
AND THE NEBRASKA
SWINDLE

JOVE BOOKS, NEW YORK

SLOCUM AND THE NEBRASKA SWINDLE

A Jove Book / published by arrangement with
the author

PRINTING HISTORY
Jove edition / January 2003

Copyright © 2003 by Penguin Putnam Inc.

Visit our website at
www.penguinputnam.com

ISBN: 0-515-13441-4

A JOVE BOOK®
Jove Books are published by The Berkley Publishing Group, a division of Penguin Putnam Inc., 375 Hudson Street, New York, New York 10014. JOVE and the "J" design are trademarks belonging to Penguin Putnam Inc.

PRINTED IN THE UNITED STATES OF AMERICA

10 9 8 7 6 5 4 3 2 1

1

"Them prairie rattlers are still comin' after us, Slocum," grumbled Big Ben London. The mountain of a man swung about in the saddle, spat, wiped his face, pulled the broad brim of his dusty Stetson down to shade his eyes, then pointed angrily, as if John Slocum had not seen the posse following them.

"They'll keep their distance," Slocum said with more assurance than he felt. His hand drifted to the ebony handle of the Colt Navy slung in a cross-draw holster, then moved away. The distance was too great, and shooting at men who sought trouble accomplished nothing. Besides, heat and exhaustion made it all too easy for Slocum to jump to conclusions. He doubted the men dogging their tracks were peaceable, but so far they had not made any move against the herd or the cowboys tending it.

The Kansas prairie was scorching hot for this time of year and the rivers had been low, thanks to drought that seemed never-ending. That had been both good and bad for the herd Slocum brought up from Abilene, Texas, for Leonard Larkin. He had met Larkin over a poker table six months earlier and had taken an immediate liking to the man. Only when the game was over did Slocum find out that Larkin was one of the biggest cattle ranchers in Abilene.

He had liked Larkin and Larkin had taken a fancy to Slocum, offering him a job as cowboy. All spring long Slocum had worked the range, keeping the cattle safe from rustlers, tending their diseases, and finally branding the new calves. By then Larkin had made Slocum top hand and had given him authority to trail boss the herd to market.

That had been the easy part, working in the breezy, dusty spring, then in the building heat of a full-fledged Texas summer. Risking his life on the trail, saving not only his right-hand man Big Ben London from drowning, but a quarter of the herd as well, when they got bogged down crossing the Red River, even fighting off a band of Comanches who refused to surrender—all that had been easy compared to trying to sell the herd.

Every now and then whispers of Texas fever spread like wildfire through the Kansas cattle towns. This was one of those years. Slocum had tried to sell the herd in Wichita and had danged near gotten lynched. It didn't matter how much he tried to explain that Larkin's herd was free of splenic fever—the disease the Kansans derogatorily called Texas fever—because they were dead set against buying any beef from down south.

Big Ben and several of the others in Slocum's crew had wanted to fight it out, but Slocum saw the futility of that. Not only was there a passel of Wichita citizens opposed to buying the herd, the law was beginning to look a bit edgy. Slocum wasn't about to go against a half dozen flinty-eyed deputies carrying sawed-off shotguns everywhere they patrolled.

He had moved the herd through Wichita on north to Salina.

The reception there had been even less hospitable. The men now dogging their trail had argued over killing and burning all the cattle rather than just driving them out of town. Slocum considered Larkin his friend and wouldn't allow the loss of the entire herd. Even if he hadn't much cottoned to Larkin, he worked for the man and had been entrusted with getting the best price for the beeves. Seeing them shoved into a big pit and burned offended Slocum, especially since he knew there wasn't a diseased cow in the herd.

Not one. But the citizens of Salina wouldn't accept the word of a dusty, hard-looking trail boss.

"I hope to hell and gone that you're right, Slocum," Big Ben said. He wiped sweat off his face with a big blue bandanna, never taking his eyes off the men on their trail. "The scrawny one—Jackson they called him—had the look of a man with religious convictions. And his religion is callin' fer the total destruction of all Texas beeves."

"We need water for the herd," Slocum said. Usually, he would have ridden ahead to scout the route and to find a place to bed down for the night, but now he wanted to keep the volatile Big Ben away from the back of the herd and any stragglers. "Go on and see what you can find."

"All right, Slocum, if that's the way you want it. But mark my words, them yahoos ain't gonna let us go. They're up to something."

"I'll watch them," Slocum promised. Big Ben grunted, cursed under his breath about flatlanders and the breeding habits of anyone living in a Kansas cow town, then urged his tired mare forward to find the water so desperately needed by the herd.

Slocum took a slow pull of tepid water from his canteen, and noted that more than the cattle needed a watering hole. The troubles in Wichita and Salina hadn't afforded him and his men much time to stock up on supplies or water. They had been lucky to get away without being strung up.

He put his heels to his roan's flanks and got the powerful stallion galloping to cut off a few cows trying to head out on their own. Slocum got in front of them, shouted a bit to get their attention and to vent his own anger at the Kansans, then got the cows moving back to the main body of the herd. As he returned to his place, eating dust from two thousand hooves kicking up the dry Kansas prairie, Slocum hung back to watch the posse behind them. He didn't like the way the six men galloped off to the east and headed out as if they intended to flank the herd. Acting as escort away from Salina was one thing. This maneuver struck Slocum as downright hostile, in spite of the posse disappearing eastward.

Slocum got the roan into a canter that soon brought him to the front of the herd. He waved to Big Ben and caught the man's attention.

"What's the trouble, Slocum?"

"Is there anything ahead that might cause us trouble?"

Big Ben shrugged. Then he frowned a mite and chewed on his lip.

"There might be somethin'," he said. "I've spent 'nough time on the prairie to recognize the way gullies get cut by heavy rain. There might be a powerful big cut in the ground ahead from the way the land rises up here. But that don't mean there's water ahead."

Slocum's mind raced. He considered the possibility that the six men who had trailed them for days were finally giving up. If they were, why didn't they turn around and go back south to Salina? They were plotting something, and it wasn't likely to be anything Slocum wanted to see.

"Turn the herd," Slocum said. "Get them moving due east."

"But that'll take us off the route, if we want to get to Nebraska," protested Big Ben.

"I think the posse'll try to stampede the herd westward," Slocum said.

"But that would drive the beeves into the gully runnin'

to the north for a dozen miles or more," Big Ben said. His eyes widened when he figured out what Slocum already had. "That damn gulch's so deep the cattle would fall into it and break their fool necks. There wouldn't be any way we could turn the herd in time."

Big Ben didn't stick around to discuss the situation further. He sawed on his horse's reins and went off at a gallop, shouting orders to the outriders to turn the herd. Slocum hoped he was doing the right thing. If the six Kansans only wanted to hurrah the herd, they would find themselves staring at two thousand head of charging cattle. But if they intended to set fire to the tinder-dry prairie, Slocum was sending the herd to certain destruction. There would be no way he could keep the cattle from rushing headlong into a raging inferno.

Good sense dictated care in setting any fire on this dry prairie, but fear of Texas fever did strange things to men. Fire might seem the perfect way to get rid of a diseased herd, even if it meant half the state would go up in greasy black smoke.

"Hi-yaaaa!" shouted Slocum. He pulled free his lariat and began using it, still coiled, to swat at the rumps of incensed cattle. The beeves had been strolling along in the hot sunlight, content to move in a straight line. Now Slocum demanded they amble off at a right angle, up a slight slope. The cattle complained loudly about it, but when Slocum reached the top of the low rise, he was glad he had ordered his trail hands to change the direction taken by the herd.

The six Kansans were spaced about a hundred yards apart, each with a rifle pulled from a saddle sheath. The sudden sight of the cattle topping the rise spooked one. He fired. This caused a reaction like a string of firecrackers going off. The man next to him fired, and the next and the next, until all six fired wildly. The first shots went into the air. Then they saw the herd begin to gather momentum—toward them.

Slocum was a bit slow to act when it became apparent the Kansans had achieved their goal of stampeding the herd. The beeves thundered down the far side of the slope directly for the six men.

"Turn the herd," Slocum shouted over the roaring earthquake caused by the stampede. "Get them moving north again!" He tried using his rope on the cattle but fear now held them too firmly. Each hemp blow fell on half a ton of frightened cow, to no avail.

Slocum looked up and saw the six men had given up firing, realizing they could never bring down enough cattle to save them. They hightailed it east, trying to keep in front of the herd.

Slocum felt nothing but contempt for the men and would have let the stampede follow them all the way to New York, if he hadn't had a duty to Len Larkin. He put his spurs to his roan's flanks and shot ahead faster than the fastest cow. Keeping his head down, he passed the leaders of the herd still charging blindly. Slocum knew the danger but did what he saw to be his job.

If he fell or his horse faltered, eight thousand hooves would trample him. Slocum slowed the roan until it was racing along at the same speed as the lead steer. When he was certain the steer had him in sight, Slocum pulled a bit on the reins and got the roan angling off to the northeast. The steer and all the others behind followed. Slocum felt the stallion under him beginning to tire but could not stop now. To do so would throw both him and his horse under those flashing, deadly bovine hooves.

He veered a little more to the north. The steers followed. He slowed a mite, uneasily judging the distance between his horse's rump and the swinging horns of the lead steer. He wished Larkin had polled the cattle, but that would have taken more work. All Slocum could do now was watch the distance narrow between the long horns and his horse.

But as the gap closed, the beeves began to calm down. They weren't as intent on a headlong frightened rush now. The six men firing their rifles had stopped, and cattle had short memories. Slocum slowed a bit more, risking a horn in the flank of his horse. The roan's eyes showed white all around. It was as frightened as the cattle had been.

As they *had been*. Slocum noted the way they were slowing, tired out from their escapade. He let his horse widen the interval between them after it became apparent the cattle were settling down.

He finally drew rein and sat on his stallion, sweat pouring off him. His shirt was glued to his body, and his eyes stung from the salty perspiration flooding off his brow. Slocum mopped at it as Big Ben London rode up.

"That was about the smartest—and dumbest—thing I ever did see. I'd wanted to be trail boss and was pissed off somethin' royal when Mr. Larkin put you in charge." Big Ben stared at Slocum for a moment, then thrust out his big paw of a hand. "I'll follow you anywhere you say, Slocum. Anywhere, anytime. I'd never have had the smarts to use the herd against them sidewinders in the first place, and I sure as hell has demons would never have tried stoppin' the stampede all by my lonesome."

Slocum shook the man's hamlike hand.

"You find that water yet?" Slocum asked. "I need a bath something fierce."

For a moment, Big Ben looked surprised, then he burst out laughing.

"Ain't found the water, but for you I surely will, even if I got to piss up into the clouds to get a rainstorm started."

"Don't go doing anything like that on my score," Slocum said, laughing. He felt exhausted from the day's ride but knew there wouldn't be any rest until they found the water and settled the herd for the night.

And maybe there wouldn't be any rest, even then, unless the Kansans had given up and gone home.

North Platte, Nebraska, didn't look much different from Salina or Wichita. The people eyed Slocum and his riders suspiciously as they rode in, the herd just outside town limits. There was no question in anyone's mind why the drovers had come to North Platte. Slocum just hoped he could talk sense to a buyer.

"Don't go whooping it up until after the ink's dry on the bill of sale," Slocum called to Big Ben and three of the cowboys who had come into town with him. "After that, I'll get you paid off and you can go where you like."

"I'd like to find myself a cathouse," Big Ben said, rubbing his crotch. "If I got anything left to show, after six weeks on the trail."

"You'd be better off buying a decent saddle," joked another of the cowboys. "I rode as far as you and I don't have no trouble. None at all. Might be yer gettin' a mite too old to pleasure the ladies."

"You young whippersnapper, why, I . . ."

Slocum left them joshing one another as he went into the small, close office. The heat outside was bad. Inside was a dozen times worse. It smelled as if something had died in the heat, but the man behind the big littered desk was too busy to notice it. He scribbled madly on one sheet of paper, moved it to a small stack and took another from a taller stack beside it.

"Afternoon," Slocum greeted when it became apparent the man wasn't going to look up or otherwise acknowledge Slocum's presence. "You the boss around here?"

"As good as anybody," the man said, finally looking up. His forehead looked like a bit of prairie had been plowed up, leaving behind leathery wrinkles the color of sod. Beady, dark eyes peered up at Slocum from behind half-glasses. As he moved, the celluloid collar constricting his neck crinkled and snapped. Slocum wondered if it held the man's head on. It appeared to be too tight for weather like this, but the man took no notice.

"I've got two thousand head of longhorns for sale. Prime stock, a little worn from the trail since there's not much grass this year, but firm flesh, healthy and ready to be sent east to the slaughterhouse."

"Porterhouses on the hoof," the man grumbled. He threw down his pen. "Rumor has it your herd's filthy with Texas fever."

"Rumor's wrong," Slocum insisted. A touch of anger entered his tone. He was fed up with the lies about Texas herds spreading the deadly disease. "You can have any vet you like examine them. No ticks, no splenic fever. Nothing that keeps them from all being prime cattle."

"Not interested. Get them out of North Platte and take them somewhere else."

"Where?" demanded Slocum.

"Not my concern. Anywhere else. Somewhere that doesn't mind having cattle falling over with fever on their doorsteps."

"The cattle are healthy. You pick the vet, I'll pay for him."

This perked up the buyer.

"That's a generous offer and one I don't hear much. What else you willing to pay for if I take these scrawny runts off your hands?"

"Depends on the price per head for these fine Texas longhorns," Slocum countered.

The man started to speak but clamped his mouth shut when a well-dressed man entered the small office.

Slocum gave him the once-over and decided this was the man he had to convince, not the clerk behind the desk.

"My name's Slocum and I have a herd to sell," he said,

thrusting out his hand. The man recoiled as if Slocum's hand had been dipped in rattlesnake venom.

"I just got a telegram from Salina. You come up from there with your herd?"

"I was tellin' him, Mr. O'Malley, how we wasn't buyin' any—"

"Shut up," O'Malley snapped. "My friends in Salina say you have a herd filthy with disease."

Slocum held his temper and repeated his offer of paying for any veterinarian O'Malley might choose to examine the herd. Again, this drove a wedge between the man's prejudices and appealed to his greed.

"Can't pay much. No water or feed. Winter was bad for taking down our supplies of fodder. Drought this summer."

"North Platte's on the railroad and you could have all the cattle on their way to Chicago within a couple days," Slocum said.

"We'd need to fatten them. Costs too much."

"Nonsense, Mr. O'Malley," cut in a soft voice. "You just bought that load of grain and don't know what to do with it. Why don't you feed it to this gentleman's cattle, fatten the beeves, then get top dollar for them from the slaughterhouse?"

"Miss Abigail, didn't hear you come up," O'Malley said, looking confused now. He didn't know whether to continue dickering with Slocum or to expend his full attention on the comely woman.

Slocum had been on the trail for six weeks, but he didn't think it was not seeing a woman for so long that made this one seem especially stunning. A small, petite blonde, she boldly faced O'Malley, firm chin set and eyes bluer than the Nebraska summer sky boring into him. She wore expensive clothing—and Slocum couldn't help noticing how well she filled it out.

"Miss Abigail?" he said.

"Abigail Stanley," she said, holding her hand out for him. Slocum almost took it and kissed it, then decided it was better to forget the gallantry for the moment and simply shook it. Abigail looked amused at his choice.

"Miss Abigail, this is business and—"

"And you are screwing it up, as usual, Mr. O'Malley. I heard him say that he didn't mind having Doc Ruggles look at his cattle."

"That's cuz he don't know Doc Ruggles," spoke up the clerk. "He's the pickiest vet this side of the Mississippi."

"Let him look twice," Slocum said. "Those beeves are clean."

"Disease free, perhaps," Abigail said, smiling, "but clean? After being on the trail?" She looked at him and wrinkled her pug nose.

"Water's been scarce, ma'am," Slocum said.

"Do call me . . . Miss Stanley," she said, smiling.

"Well?" demanded Slocum. "Thirty dollars a head is a fine price for such good beef on the hoof."

"Thirty?" O'Malley replied. "Outrageous. Not a cent over twenty, unless Doc Ruggles gives a clean bill of health. And maybe not then."

"Let's look at the herd," Slocum said.

"Very well." O'Malley left the office and didn't hear Abigail whisper to Slocum.

"He'll pay twenty-eight dollars a head. You should have started at forty."

"Thank you for your help, Miss Stanley," Slocum said.

She grinned broader. "My pleasure, and you can call me Abigail." She turned with a swish of her skirts, shot him a broad grin and left.

Slocum couldn't take his eyes off his lovely benefactor. Behind him he heard the clerk mutter, "Damnation. She never looked at me that way."

Slocum hurried out, intent on completing the deal with O'Malley so he could buy Abigail Stanley dinner at someplace decent in town to thank her for her help.

2

The balding veterinarian pushed his spectacles back up his nose, rubbed his hands on his shiny trousers, then stepped back, struck a pose and told O'Malley, "These are 'bout the finest beeves I ever laid eyes on. Most cattle of this quality get bought up down in Kansas 'fore they get this far north. If you buy the herd, Jimmy, I want a steak off that one." Doc Ruggles pointed to a steer with bulging sides.

Slocum shook his head in wonder at how the steer had managed to remain so plump during the hard trip from Texas, but he wasn't going to say anything aloud. The vet pretty well sold O'Malley on the herd's health, and by adding the comment about wanting a slice of beef off one, he clinched the deal.

"They're everything you said they were, Mr. Slocum," O'Malley said. "But the price. Too expensive. Can't make a profit 'less I sell them for twice what I pay you." He shook his head and looked sideways at Slocum, as if judging how long such a lie could stand before he had to up his offer to something more reasonable.

"They're fine Texas longhorns," insisted Slocum. The two got down to serious dickering. Slocum didn't get as high a price as Abigail Stanley had suggested, but O'Malley agreed to pay Doc Ruggles for his services as part of the deal. Getting rid of the herd after being run out of two Kansas cow towns made Slocum feel mighty happy at the moment. He was willing to trade a couple dollars a head for successfully closing the transaction.

"How do you want to get paid?" O'Malley asked.

Slocum did some quick figuring. He had to pay off Big Ben London and the rest of the crew for their month and a half on the trail. The cook got a bonus for not poisoning any of them along the way, and Leonard Larkin had trusted Slocum enough with the herd to give him a percentage of the profits.

"Eight hundred dollars cash, the rest wired to Mr. Larkin down in Abilene," Slocum said.

"You can tend to that chore over at the bank. We got 'bout the finest bank manager in all Nebraska. You can trust him with your life." O'Malley snorted and then added, "I do more than that. I trust him with my money."

Slocum and O'Malley went to the bank, drew up the papers and completed the transaction.

"You and your crew can move the beeves into the pens. You owe me that much, me giving you such a princely sum," O'Malley said.

Slocum wasn't going to argue.

"I need to speak to the trail hands before letting them ride their separate trails, anyway," Slocum said. He hesitated and O'Malley caught it.

"Something more, Mr. Slocum? Something eating you?"

"I was wondering where I might find Miss Stanley. I owe her a meal for helping interest you in buying the herd."

O'Malley laughed and slapped Slocum on the back. "She'll turn up, if she wants to see you again. Nobody's ever gonna put a brand on that filly. She's one wild mustang." The man hurried off to the telegraph station to send a wire east to find a buyer for the cattle. He might have to fatten the cattle for a week or more until the train arrived to take the beeves off his hands, but every extra pound meant more money for him. North Platte wasn't on the regular railroad route for moving beeves, and he might have to arrange for a special train. But it would be worth it to him and to whatever company bought Larkin's steers.

Slocum didn't begrudge O'Malley his undoubtedly hefty profit. He and Big Ben and the rest of the trail crew had moved the cattle a considerable ways, but they were being paid for it. And Len Larkin would get enough money to bring another herd north next year. Slocum hoped the citizens of the cow towns in Kansas wouldn't be as skittish about infected cattle then.

He considered returning to Abilene and working for Larkin another year. The man was a decent employer and the pay was adequate, but Slocum was starting to get a little antsy. Being trail boss was as good as it would ever get working for a rancher, not that Slocum hankered to have a spread of his own.

That would tie him down too much.

He stepped out into the dusty North Platte street and took a deep whiff. The various aromas mingled in a heady miasma. Horses and cattle. Garbage and dust. Things alive and dead. But under it all ran the smell, the taste, the feel of too many people crowding together. Slocum wanted to ride west into the Rockies and spend the summer in a high country park where the air was clean and his only neighbor was a grizzly in the next valley over.

But before he lit out, he wanted to spend a little time with Abigail Stanley. She was as pretty as they came, and he did owe her something for pushing O'Malley into considering purchase of the herd.

He went to the pens, bellowed for Big Ben and the rest.

It took the better part of the afternoon getting the cattle into the feedlots and making certain that any stragglers were rounded up and brought in. Slocum would never cheat Len Larkin—nor would he short Jim O'Malley of even one head of cattle that he had purchased.

"Gather round," Slocum said, perching on the top rail of the corral. He began paying out the men's hard earned money. Most got $50 in silver for their work. He made sure Big Ben got paid off in gold.

"What about me?" whined the cook.

"I ought to bury your body out on the prairie so you won't give anybody else a bellyache from your cooking," Slocum joked. He paid the cook a mix of gold and silver coins. It took the portly man a few seconds to count the money. He finally tallied all the coins in his dirty hand and looked up, a gold tooth in the front of his mouth flashing in the sunlight.

"I'm right obliged, Slocum. Anytime you want me to pizzen you and your crew, you jist ask."

"Mr. Larkin wouldn't mind seeing you boys riding herd on the Lazy L brand again," Slocum told them.

"You headin' back that way, Slocum?" asked Big Ben. "If you are, I reckon I can, too."

"Right now, all I intend doing is finding a saloon where I can wet my whistle."

"North Platte's full of gin mills," Big Ben declared. "Why don't you start at one end of town and I'll start at the other? I'll race you through 'em all!"

This brought a cheer of encouragement from the other cowboys. Slocum walked slower than the rest of them and soon found himself alone in the street. That suited him fine. He wasn't much for goodbyes. A drink or two would be all he needed. If Abigail Stanley turned up somewhere during his drinking spree, fine. If she didn't, he was already making plans for leaving Nebraska.

Slocum went up the steps to the tall front doors of the

Hangman's Noose Saloon. Not much noise came from inside, but he saw several locals bellied up to the bar. If the natives drank here, it had to be all right. He went in and ordered a shot of whiskey.

"Two bits," the barkeep said. Slocum laid down a half dollar and got a second shot standing beside the first. He stared at them for a moment, anticipating how they would taste. On the trail he had drunk bad water and worse whiskey, and he wanted these shots to go down easy and match the best he'd ever sampled.

He quickly downed the first and felt the satisfying warmth searing its way to his belly, where it pooled. Slocum licked the rim of the shot glass to capture every last amber drop, then set it down on the bar with a loud click.

"Good," he declared. He turned and put his elbows on the bar, saving the second drink until the first had settled down a mite. Slocum's green eyes narrowed when he saw a poker game at a table toward the rear of the saloon. He pushed up his Stetson to get a better look.

"Anything wrong, mister?" asked the barkeep, seeing his interest—and the way he had stiffened.

"You know that gent? The tinhorn gambler across the table from the two prosperous-looking men?"

"Sure do. He blowed into town like a Kansas tornado nigh on a week ago. Name's Rafe Ferguson. He a friend of yours?"

"I wouldn't go that far," Slocum said.

"Hold on, mister. The Hangman's Noose is a respectable place. You got a bone to pick with him, you take it out back!"

"It's not like that," Slocum said, settling down. He sipped at the second whiskey. It didn't taste quite as good as the first, but then it never did. If he ordered a third drink, he wouldn't taste it at all.

"How is it, then? Like I said, I don't let nobody bust up my place."

"Ferguson's a crooked gambler. I was wondering if I ought to warn the men in the game with him."

"How do you come to know him?" The saloon owner scowled at Slocum.

"He tried cheating me down at Fort Griffin, down in Texas. But then all the gamblers in Fort Griffin were cheats." Slocum eyed the two nattily dressed men in the game with Ferguson. They looked well enough heeled to take any loss the crooked gambler might hand them. It certainly didn't look as if they or their families would starve if Rafe Ferguson walked away with their entire pokes.

"He might do a little bottom dealing, but nuthin' I ever caught him at," the saloon owner said. "You're not fixin' to cause a ruckus?"

"No reason to," Slocum said. "I might warn those gents about Ferguson being a swindler, too. He came up with some mighty crazy schemes and got even crazier people to invest in them. He cleaned them all out once he had their gold riding in his saddlebags."

"Not my concern. Don't make it none of yours, neither," the barkeep said. "You got any problem with Ferguson, you tell it to the marshal. He runs a peaceable town here."

Slocum had always wondered why glancing at a man or talking about him seemed to alert the man to danger. Slocum had spoken enough of how Ferguson was a crook to reach the point where the gambler swung about nervously in his straight-backed wood chair and locked eyes with Slocum.

Rafe Ferguson jumped to his feet as if he had been stuck with a pin. When he saw that Slocum wasn't going to throw down on him, he looked left and right, then bolted for the rear door.

"The wicked fleeth when no man pursues," Slocum said.

"Don't that beat all? He caught sight of you and lit out like a jackrabbit." The barkeep went back to polishing shot glasses, but he kept a sharp eye on Slocum to see what he would do.

Slocum finished the last of the whiskey, put it down softly on the bar and considered ordering another. Then he got to wondering what had spooked Rafe Ferguson so much. They had not parted on good terms, but if Slocum had been really riled, he would have tracked the son of a bitch down and settled accounts then and there.

He wasn't the kind of man, if he had gotten bit, to let a snake like Ferguson slither off, then track him down a couple years later. Slocum took care of business right away, and never looked back. Yet the way the gambler had acted bespoke of a guilty conscience—and not simply from using a marked deck in the poker game with Slocum.

Slocum ran his finger around the rim of the shot glass, tasted the last drop of whiskey and then pushed away from the bar. The saloon owner jumped back, as if he expected Slocum to clear leather and start shooting. Walking slowly, Slocum went to the rear door Ferguson had used and poked his head out warily. He didn't want the gambler shooting him because he got careless.

Ferguson hurried along, his shiny boots kicking up small clouds of dust. Slocum knew he ought to let the matter lie. He had no quarrel with Ferguson that amounted to a hill of beans, but his curiosity was getting the better of him. He had been devoted to herding cattle for too long and considered tracking down Ferguson a diversion. Long strides took him down behind the buildings to the corner where Ferguson had disappeared.

Slocum had been cautious leaving the Hangman's Noose Saloon but thought the gambler was on the run. He didn't expect the attack that came at him when he rounded the corner.

A heavy log swinging for his face caused him to duck

instinctively and dodge. The wood grazed the top of his head and staggered him, before crashing into the side of the building with a resounding crack. If it had hit him full-on, he would have been knocked out.

"Who're you?" Slocum called, stumbling back as he recovered his senses. He had thought Ferguson was the club wielder, but the man in front of him was hard of face and roughly dressed. Behind him came up a second man, equally tough-looking.

"Go on, Slocum, go for the hogleg," called Rafe Ferguson, standing behind the two men. "I want a reason to cut you down where you stand."

"You've got no call to shoot me, Ferguson," said Slocum. "What's this about?"

Slocum found talking wasn't what the two men had in mind. They both rushed him. He swung clumsily and hit one, knocking him aside. But Slocum was off balance and fell against the building, leaving him wide open for the second man's attack. Strong arms circled his waist and carried him back. The two of them fell to the ground, flailing about. Neither was able to land a solid punch.

Finally twisting around, Slocum got to his hands and knees with the man behind him. As the man approached him, Slocum kicked out like a mule. His foot landed smack in the middle of the man's belly, doubling him over. But the first man surged at Slocum again, this time brandishing a knife with a long, wickedly shining blade.

"You're gonna die," the man said.

Slocum rolled to get away, came to his feet and went for his Colt Navy. He drew his six-shooter, cocked and fired in one smooth motion. A cloud of white smoke momentarily blocked the attacker from Slocum's view, then he saw the result of his quick shot.

The man fell to one knee, clutching his other thigh. Blood oozed out between his fingers and drenched his denim jeans. He looked up, pure hatred in his piglike eyes.

"I'm gonna kill you for this, Slocum."

"You had your chance," Slocum said coldly. He cocked his six-gun again, but before he could aim it he heard another, more ominous sound.

The noise a double-barreled shotgun makes when both hammers are pulled back was too distinctive for Slocum to ignore.

"You jist point that smoke wagon of yours in some other direction. Like down at the ground. I got a shotgun aimed at yer back and I'll cut you in half if you so much as twitch."

"Ferguson has bought himself quite a gang," Slocum said, doing as he was told. There was a time to fight and a time to talk. He could only die now if he tried to shoot it out.

"Don't know no Ferguson, sonny, but I seen what I seen. You shot that feller."

"He was coming at me with a knife. See? There, on the ground."

"It's not mine!" the wounded man cried. "He musta dropped it. He shot me and threw down the knife to make it look like I was tryin' to cut him."

Slocum said nothing. If the man behind didn't work for Ferguson, the truth would be obvious. There was no call to plant a weapon if he could fire a second time and finish off his assailant.

"Why don't we all mosey on down the street to the jail? I'll let the marshal sort this out. I ain't paid enough to do that chore."

Slocum stepped forward and put his foot on the knife as Ferguson's henchman grabbed for it.

"Let him carry it," Slocum said coldly.

"A right good idea, mister. And I'll take that six-gun of yers, too."

Slocum let the deputy take the gun from his grip, then pick up the knife and tuck it into his belt. The badge shining dully on the man's vest confirmed Slocum's suspicion about what had happened. The owner of the saloon had sent for the law the instant Slocum left.

"I can't walk," whined the injured man, hobbling more than he had to so he could garner some sympathy. Slocum wanted to kick his other leg out from under him, but he didn't budge.

"You might offer to help him," the deputy said.

"I might," Slocum said, not moving a muscle.

"Get a-walkin', you two," the deputy said, realizing he had a pair of hard cases in his sights.

Slocum seethed as he went toward the calaboose at the far end of town. Rafe Ferguson ought to be the one with the shotgun pointed at his spine. But by the time Slocum went into the small jailhouse, he had calmed down enough to avoid the pitfall too many cowboys fell into: Arguing with the marshal and calling him names was a sure ticket to the iron-barred cells lining the rear of the office. If he wanted to get out of North Platte without spending a week in the lockup, Slocum had to be persuasive.

"What we got here, Jed?"

"Fenstermacher at the Hangman's Noose warned me there was gonna be trouble. I caught this one pointin' this at that one." The deputy dropped Slocum's Colt Navy on the marshal's desk, then added the knife.

"He tried to murder me!" blurted the wounded man. "See? He shot me!"

"That the way it happened?" asked the marshal. Slocum wasn't certain who the lawman was speaking to, so he held his tongue. The deputy spoke up.

"Can't really say, Marshal. Got there too late for anything but stoppin' what would have been a killin'."

"Lock them both up for a week. Disturbing the peace."

"Don't put me in the same cell with him! He tried to kill me once already today. Now that I'm sorely wounded, he'll murder me for sure!"

"Shut up," the marshal said without rancor. He motioned to the deputy to lock up his prisoner in the end cell. The lawman ran his fingers over the worn ebony handle of Slocum's six-shooter, then picked it up, cocked it and listened to the way the sensitive mechanism worked.

"You put a lot of time in maintainin' this here weapon, don't you?"

"It keeps me alive."

"You've used it a lot, too," the marshal said. "You aren't a professional gunman, are you?"

"I brought in a herd from Texas. Just sold it to Mr. O'Malley."

"Did you now? So you get likkered up and go out shooting men? Or did you have a quarrel with him?" The marshal jerked his thumb over his shoulder in the direction of the cell.

"Don't even know who he is. I wanted to talk with an old acquaintance named Rafe Ferguson. I trailed him out of the saloon and was set upon by that owlhoot and another one."

"That true, Jedediah? You see a second—or third—gent out there?"

"Nope, Marshal, these two was the only ones I seen."

"Any reason I shouldn't lock you up?"

"He tried to kill me, Marshal!" shouted the prisoner. "Don't let him walk out of here a free man!"

"He came at me with the knife."

"Shut up," the deputy said before his prisoner could protest further. To the marshal, Jed said, "It don't seem too plausible that that gent would drop a knife between shootin's. The knife prob'ly belongs to this one and the one with the gun was only defendin' hisself."

"Jed's a shrewd observer, but this needs sortin' out when the judge gets back from ridin' his circuit," the marshal said.

"So you're going to lock me up?" asked Slocum.

"Reckon so." The marshal had stood, ready to escort Slocum to the cells, when the sunlight coming through the open office door suddenly darkened. And then the light swept into the dingy room.

"Why, Marshal Durant, you know the facts. I heard part of what you were saying and I am sure you have it right. Mr. Slocum was only defending himself from that ruffian."

"Miss Stanley," the marshal said, grinning like an idiot.

Slocum stepped back and let Abigail Stanley talk him out of his jam. Before he knew it, he was following her outside into the hot Nebraska sun, a free man.

3

"That's twice I have to thank you," Slocum said, moving closer to Abigail as she walked briskly down the boardwalk. The alternating flashes of sunlight and shadow on her face turned her into some exotic creature that thrilled Slocum. He tried to keep from staring but couldn't do it. The petite blonde never looked at him as she bustled along, occasionally greeting the merchants and their customers coming and going from the stores.

"You look to know everyone in town," Slocum said. "But I get the feeling you don't live in North Platte."

"That's very astute. Why do you say that?"

"From what O'Malley said, he would have homed in on you like an eagle going after a field mouse if you had been a resident."

Abigail laughed and it was like silver bells ringing. She locked her arm through his and never broke step.

"O'Malley is married. I would never have anything to do with a married man." For the first time she cast a sultry look in Slocum's direction. "Are you married, John?"

"Nope," he said. From the slender-fingered hand resting on his arm, he saw she didn't wear a wedding ring. "Neither are you. Why not?"

"Why, John, that's such an impertinent question. I certainly don't owe you an answer, but I will give you one, nonetheless." For a moment she sounded like a schoolmarm lecturing her students. But no schoolmarm Slocum had ever seen was this pretty. "I have a destiny to fulfill, and that involves building my hometown into the biggest, best city in all Nebraska."

"North Platte is pretty good sized," Slocum said, "but then you don't live here, do you? Where do you hail from?"

Abigail hesitated a moment, and Slocum thought she was going to lie. Then she pulled herself up straighter and said, "No Consequence."

It took him a second to realize that was the name of her town.

"No Consequence, Nebraska?"

"You've heard of it?" she asked hopefully. Then Abigail's expression melted a little when she realized he hadn't. "That's the problem. It is a wonderful place to live and work, but without a railroad, we'll never amount to a hill of beans. North Platte has a railroad line. But No Consequence will have a spur line soon."

"You come to North Platte often to do business?" Slocum guessed. The way the citizens knew and respected her, that had to be the answer.

"Only once a month or so, but it is enough to get to know these fine people. I've even extended invitations to some of the people to move to No Consequence. So far, none have taken me up on it, but that's going to change."

"When the railroad line gets to No Consequence," Slocum finished for her.

"Yes," she said, a flush coming to her cheeks. Slocum had seen religious fervor before and this was it. Abigail was passionate about putting her town on the map. He wondered what else she was passionate about.

It didn't take long to find out.

"Do come up to my hotel room, John," she invited. "I have so much to show you."

"What might that be?" he asked.

Abigail batted her eyelashes at him and tried to look coy. Instead she looked more bold, especially when she licked her lips and squeezed a mite harder on his arm.

"Oh, maps and plans and . . . things."

"I like things," Slocum said, letting her guide him into the hotel. He had not realized they were blocking the front door of the three-story hotel until she turned and got him moving inside.

"Hello, Miss Abigail," greeted the clerk. His eyebrows arched slightly when he saw Slocum was accompanying her, but he said nothing more. Slocum could read the man's mind. Pure envy flowed forth.

Abigail Stanley hurried up the stairs, holding her skirts higher than she needed to. Slocum caught a glimpse of her fine ankles and lovely tapering legs as she turned at the top of the stairs. Looking up at her made him catch his breath in anticipation. Her firm, pert breasts jutted out nicely, their size emphasized by her tiny waist.

Abigail stared at him and him alone as she reached up and unbuttoned the top of her blouse. He started to warn her about someone seeing, then stopped. The stunning blonde knew what she was doing—and he was the only one who could see as she continued to unbutton her blouse until it lay open. Frilly ruffled undergarments hid her firm breasts but not for long. Abigail fumbled a couple times and then pulled free the satin ribbons holding everything in place.

Her garments fell away, leaving her naked to the waist.

Slocum stared at her firm white breasts capped with tiny nubs of coral. He fancied he could see them pulse with every beat of her heart as they hardened with lust for him. Three quick strides, taking the steps two at a time, brought him up to a spot two steps lower than Abigail. His mouth was on a level with her chest.

He bent forward because this seemed to be what she wanted. Abigail sighed softly when his mouth engulfed her left breast. His tongue began laving the sleek slopes, and when he came to the hard nipple at the top, he closed his lips firmly around it and suckled.

"Oh, John, yes," she said, sagging slightly. Abigail reached out and laced her fingers behind his head to hold it in place. He wasn't going anywhere, although being in public like this made him a little uneasy. Then Slocum realized it also excited him as much as it did Abigail. She had a reputation to lose and was willing to risk it by this open dalliance.

He pushed his head back against her entrapping fingers and moved to the other delicate cone. He started at the base and slowly spiraled his way to the crest, taking his time and letting his rough tongue dish out incredible excitement to the woman as he worked upward. He caught the rubbery nubbin in his teeth and lightly bit.

This time Abigail's knees did buckle. Slocum caught her easily, but she wasn't going to let him carry her off to her room. Not yet.

"Go on," she urged, lifting her skirts. "There's nothing between me and your wonderful tongue."

Abigail hiked her skirts even more, revealing those marvelous legs Slocum had noticed before. And he quickly found that she was telling the truth. No silken or frilly undergarments kept him away from paradise. The tightly tangled blond fleece nestled between her legs was dotted with sparkling drops of her inner oils.

Slocum thrust his head under her skirts and for a moment was left in the dark. Then he worked his way up until he found the moist slit rimmed with the silken fur and gave it the best tongue lashing he could. Abigail's knees had buckled from reaction before. As he ran his mouth over her nether lips, she collapsed completely.

"I . . . I thought I could continue here. I can't. There, John, that room. Mine." She was almost incoherent as she pointed.

When Slocum scooped her up and carried her into the small room she did not protest at all. He dropped her on the bed. Her sudden weight on the creaking springs caused her to rock back and forth. Somehow, she managed to lift her skirts and again reveal the pleasures hidden from everyone else.

"Don't be shy," she said, urging him on. "I'm not."

"I noticed," Slocum said, dropping his gun belt and working on his shirt and jeans. It took him longer to get out of his boots than he liked, but Abigail was doing things to him to keep him interested—as if he would ever walk away now.

As he slid off his boots, her hands roved his back and over the myriad scars there from knife and bullet wounds. Then she worked around his waist to his crotch and firmly grabbed the organ jutting up like a flagpole.

"So big, John, so very, very big." Abigail stroked up and down its length. "You're like a stallion."

"Ready to be ridden?" he asked, turning to her and taking her in his arms.

"Ridden but never broken," she said huskily before she started nibbling on his earlobe.

Slocum felt her breasts flatten against his chest as he drew her closer. Their lips crushed passionately, and he felt as if he would explode like a young buck with his first woman. Abigail was gorgeous and she was willing and there was no sense in holding back.

He bore her down to the bed. It creaked mournfully beneath their weight as he positioned himself in the V of her slender legs. Slocum stroked over the tender flesh of her thighs and then worked higher. Abigail closed her bright blue eyes and thrashed about on the bed, her fine blond hair forming a halo around her head. His fingers worked their way into her most intimate recess. He stroked a few times and then knew he couldn't keep on like this. As much as it pleasured Abigail, it was pushing him to the limits of his endurance. He had been six weeks on the trail without a woman.

He slipped his fingers from her and then worked his hips around until the crown of his manhood poked insistently into her trembling nether lips.

"Do it, do it hard, John. I like it hard and fast and—ohhh!"

She gasped out in pleasure as he slid full-length into her. For a moment Slocum hung suspended, relishing the feel of her tightness all around him. Then he began retreating, slowly, an inch at a time until only the thick knob on the end of his shaft remained within her pinkly scalloped lips.

He looked down into the woman's passion-racked face and knew she was enjoying this lovemaking as much as he was. Slocum's hips moved of their own accord and sent him surging forward. Their crotches ground together, and Slocum felt the heat within his loins turn into a raging forest fire.

Still locked together, he bent forward and lightly lapped at her nipples, her breasts, the deep valley between. Then he worked up to her delicate throat, where a vein pulsed powerfully. He did not stop moving, licking, nipping, kissing until he once again kissed her hard on the lips.

She clawed at his back, her fingers curling into claws. This spurred him on. He began thrusting rhythmically even as he kissed Abigail. They strove together, melting into one another until Slocum found it hard to figure out where he ended and Abigail began. The heat from his loins spread throughout his body and caused sweat to bead and run in tickling rivers along his skin. Then the impossible happened. The feel of her movement under him, around him, all over him made him even harder.

"John, you fill me up so, so big, so—aieee!" She arched her back and crammed her hips against his so her crotch rubbed frantically against his. Slocum felt as if he had thrust into a mine shaft and had it collapse all around him. He was crushed flat within the moist, soft, firm, exciting female sheath. Slocum kept thrusting, moving faster, deeper, giving every thrust a little rotation as he corkscrewed his way in and out.

Abigail shrieked out her pleasure again, and this time Slocum was unable to continue. He spilled his white-hot seed as climax totally possessed him.

Slocum rocked back and got up on his knees so he could look down on the blonde. Her cheeks were flushed all the way down to the tops of her breasts. She panted heavily and tiny specks of sweat beaded like tiny jewels on her face and body. When she opened her eyes, they remained unfocused for a moment. Then she reached out to him.

"That was even better than I thought it would be," Abigail said, smiling wickedly. "And I thought it was going to be great!"

Slocum sank down beside her on the bed, holding her close. Abigail turned a little and snuggled closer. The afternoon heat made it a mite uncomfortable, but Slocum wasn't complaining. Her breasts rubbed against his bare chest and one of her slender legs lifted up and draped over his thigh so she could rub herself like a cat against his flesh.

"I certainly don't have any complaints," he said.

"No complaints! No complaints! It was the most fabulous sex ever and you don't have any complaints!"

"If I said I'd had better, would you be willing to try again?" he asked. From the way he hung limp, Slocum's mouth was making a deal his body couldn't finish.

"You're lying. You've never had it better!"

"You might be wrong," Slocum said, grinning.

"Where? Tell me all about it. And yourself. Where are you from? Georgia? Your accent sounds like you're from Georgia."

Slocum only nodded. He had left Georgia and never intended returning. During the war he had fought for the Confederacy and done things he wasn't too proud of when he rode with Quantrill's Raiders. Protesting the Lawrence, Kansas, raid where boys as young as eight were gunned down by Quantrill and Bloody Bill Anderson and the others had earned him a bullet in the belly. They had left him for dead, but he had lived, just to spite them.

When he had recovered, the war was over and he had gone back to Slocum's Stand in Calhoun, Georgia. His brother Robert had died during Pickett's Charge and his mother and father had caught cholera and never recovered. He alone was left to work the spread deeded to his family by George I—until a carpetbagger judge had taken a fancy to the land and tried to seize it because of unpaid taxes.

Slocum had left the judge and his arrogant hired gunman in shallow graves near the springhouse and had stayed ahead of wanted posters bearing his likeness ever since. Out west, no one much cared about Eastern judges, but Slocum had not led the purest of lives there, either.

"Used to live in Georgia," Slocum allowed, not willing to say much more. "I move around a lot now. There's always something new to see." He ran his hands down Abigail's bare back, then worked his way up under her skirts so he could squeeze her buttocks. "And something to do."

"Oh, John, you're incorrigible!" He noticed she wasn't shying away as he squeezed and kneaded those fleshy mounds. "Other than trail boss, have you done anything else?"

"What did you have in mind?"

"Other than putting you out to stud?" The blonde

flashed him a wicked smile. Then it softened a little. "I have several wagons of goods destined for No Consequence. There's been a considerable number of robberies lately, and I wondered if you would help guard them."

"What are the wagons carrying?"

"Things that should be brought to town by rail," she said with a touch of bitterness. "Food, clothing, nails—supplies like that. Things we need to keep going until the spur is built."

"You sound mighty confident this railroad will be constructed soon."

"It will, John, it will. We are raising money by selling municipal bonds. When we get enough, we can go to the railroad and bring the line directly across the prairie from Omaha. If we have enough money left over, we'll run a spur line down to North Platte. That'll make *us* the rail center where all commerce will flow."

"Sounds mighty ambitious," he said.

"That's the only way to live," she said breathlessly, caught up in her vision. "Why don't you join me in it, John?"

"All you need is a shotgun guard for the wagons from here to No Consequence?"

"It'll be dangerous," Abigail said. "But I'll pay top dollar. We need the supplies. If any of the men who came with you on the trail drive are interested, I might have enough extra money to hire one or two of them."

"Big Ben London might be interested," Slocum said. The man was built like a mountain and handled himself well. "If he isn't completely soused yet."

"We don't have to leave until tomorrow," she said. Abigail began rocking slowly back and forth, her legs tightening around his thigh. Slocum felt oily dampness begin to slicken his flesh and knew there was plenty of time until they left tomorrow.

Right now, they had an evening and an entire night to fill.

4

"Shore am glad you invited me along on this little jaunt, Slocum," Big Ben London said in his booming voice. He rocked back in the saddle, stretched mightily and then yawned until it looked like a cavern opening. "This is the best danged rest I ever had. And I'm gettin' paid fer it, too."

They had spent four days nursemaiding the three wagons from North Platte across dry prairie, through deep gullies and over grassland torn up by buffalo herds. If Slocum read the terrain and the map Abigail had given him right, No Consequence was less than five miles off, sitting in a slight bowl and out of sight unless he found an especially tall hill. Considering how flat the countryside was, Slocum didn't put much store in finding such a vantage point. And it didn't matter. They were almost to the town Abigail was certain would blossom and grow into a major city rivaling Kansas City or Chicago.

He looked at the blonde sitting on the hard seat of a buckboard, her eyes ahead and a look approaching rapture on her face. She was going home. That look had been caused by something different each of the nights they had been on the road to No Consequence. She and Slocum had always managed to sneak away for a midnight assignation that lasted almost until dawn. That left them tuckered out, but Slocum wasn't complaining.

From what he could tell, Abigail had nothing to complain about, either.

"Do you reckon she was makin' up stories about road agents?" asked Big Ben.

"Why would she do that?"

Big Ben laughed. "Of all folks, you ought to know the answer to that. The little lady's taken quite a fancy to you, Slocum. If you don't want her throwin' her brand on you, you'd better hightail it right now."

"It's not like that," Slocum said.

"Yeah? Where was you headed when you paid off Larkin's crew? Not north to some prairie dog hole named No Consequence."

"A detour. As you said, the money's fine." Slocum smiled broadly and added, "And the other benefits that go with the trip aren't too bad, either."

Big Ben laughed uproariously at this. Then he died.

Slocum heard the report from the rifle a heartbeat after Big Ben London toppled from his horse. The bullet had caught the big man smack in the temple, killing him instantly.

"Go on, keep driving!" Slocum shouted, waving his arms to attract the attention of the freighters. "Don't stop!"

"John, what is it?" shouted Abigail. She twisted around on the buckboard seat, looking more startled than afraid. The woman hadn't figured out that the road agents she'd feared were shooting at them.

Slocum hoped she wouldn't order the driver to halt. He pulled his Winchester from its saddle sheath and brought it around, peering into the setting sun and hoping to spot the bushwhacker who had killed Big Ben. The sun was in his eyes, but he caught movement a hundred yards off in the waist-high sere grass.

Slocum began firing methodically, trying to flush the killer. His shots went wide of their target. He started to ride in that direction, then changed his mind. If any road agents had been watching, they knew only he and Big Ben rode along as guards. The teamsters might fire a rifle or pistol if they were attacked, but more likely they would throw up their hands and surrender any cargo when faced with a six-shooter.

If the outlaws meant to lure Slocum out and catch him in a crossfire, they were going about it right. He glanced at the fallen Big Ben and knew he couldn't leave him for the buzzards. Slocum jumped to the ground, wrestled the man up and heaved him over his saddle and spent a few minutes lashing him securely so he wouldn't slide off.

"Sorry about this," Slocum muttered as he worked. He wasn't sure he and Big Ben would ever have been close friends, but he had liked the huge man and certainly had never intended for him to get dry-gulched like this.

Slocum swung back into his own saddle and fought to control his roan. The horse was still spooked from the shooting. And something more. Slocum had come to rely on the horse's acute senses; the roan now spotted movement in tall grass ahead and to the left of the route they had taken. Slocum sighted in on the spot, squeezed back on the rifle trigger and was rewarded with a yelp of pain.

He might not have killed the outlaw, but he had certainly winged him. That might put a speck of fear into the rest. Slocum spurred his horse and got it trotting, leading Big Ben's horse with its grisly load.

"Who's shooting at us, John?" shouted Abigail.

He wished she would get down and not present such a good target. Her bright golden hair gleamed in the afternoon sunlight and drew unwanted attention to her. Slocum swung around, sharp eyes looking for any sign of their attackers. Four horsemen to the west were riding at an angle to cut off the wagons.

"Ahead! Four outlaws," he shouted. Slocum kept riding, praying that there weren't more of the owlhoots lying in wait to ambush him. He reached the back of Abigail's buckboard and hitched Big Ben's horse to it.

"He—he's dead," she said, her blue eyes wide with horror. "I didn't know. They shot him? The road agents?"

"Yep," Slocum said, "and they'll shoot you unless you keep your pretty head down." To the driver he said, "Four riders are somewhere between you and No Consequence, ready to waylay you. How well do you know the country here?"

"Pretty good," the man said, looking pale under his weathered skin. "If'n they're ahead of us, we can circle and come into No Consequence from the east. But if they figger that out, catchin' us'll be a breeze."

"Not if I slow them down," Slocum said.

"John, no, don't. It's too dangerous going after them alone, especially when they're already killed your friend."

"You hired me to do a job, and I'm doing it. Get moving!"

The buckboard lurched off, the other wagons following, leaving the double ruts that passed for a road. Slocum waited for them to disappear eastward before he took a deep breath, made sure his six-shooter and rifle were fully loaded and went to stop some killers.

Slocum had done a bit of outlawry in his day, but he never killed for no reason. If the men he had robbed tried foolishly to shoot him, he had no problem shooting back—or even shooting first. But to kill a man from ambush for no reason rankled. That showed these outlaws had a streak of pure mean in them.

He trotted ahead a hundred yards and got to the top of a small, rolling hill. In the distance he saw smoke rising from chimneys in No Consequence. These men were either desperate or mighty cocky to rob Abigail within sight of her town. If they were desperate, that made them doubly dangerous.

If they were only arrogant, Slocum would see them in shallow graves before the sun set.

He looked lower, away from the smoke curling from No Consequence, and saw dust settling. Slocum started to ride for it, then reined back and reconsidered. It was foolish to shoot a guard, then expect the wagon train to ride ahead into a trap—unless the road agents had something else in mind.

Like having the remaining guard divert the wagons.

Slocum cursed under his breath, hoping he had not played into the outlaws' hands. But the dust cloud kept moving and didn't settle, as if the owlhoots were laying in wait. They kept riding to the east, on a course that would cut off Abigail and her wagons.

Galloping now, Slocum followed the wagons and quickly saw why the road agents had planned their trap the way they had. The road directly into No Consequence was relatively smooth. This way forced the wagons to go through deep ravines that slowed them.

The gunfire as Slocum raced up told him the wagons were caught at the bottom of a gully, sitting ducks for the road agents. As he galloped ahead, he worried there were too many of them to fight off. One had killed Big Ben. He had wounded another. At least four rode across the original route—had they been insurance that Slocum would send the wagons directly into this trap? If so, he might be facing another six or eight outlaws.

When he reached the lip of the ravine he saw the drivers trying to put up a fight, but they were caught between two bands of ambushers. One had let the wagons go down into the sandy-bottomed wash and the other lay in hiding ready to attack from the far rim. Both groups of outlaws fired downward from the high ground.

Slocum went to work to eliminate one side of the road agents' trap. He jumped from his horse and stalked along the rim to a spot where the tall blue grama grass parted and two rifle barrels poked out. Smoke rose from each muzzle every time the outlaws fired.

He drew his Colt Navy, took careful aim and fired. The slug missed but the sparks from the muzzle set fire to the dry grass. This was good enough to flush the two. The outlaws jumped to their feet, no longer intent on shooting at Abigail and her freighters.

"Drop 'em," Slocum said, pointing his six-shooter at a spot between the two men. They exchanged furtive glances, and Slocum knew they weren't going to surrender. He went into a crouch, shot the man on the left, then swung fast and got a shot off at the same time as the remaining outlaw.

Slocum was a better shot and lived. His target died.

He stamped out the small blaze he had caused, scooped up the two men's rifles and turned them on the far bank of the wash. When one magazine came up empty, Slocum threw down the rifle and used the second. He wasn't doing much more than kicking up tiny dust clouds with every slug, but he let the other outlaws know their prey was fighting back.

"Get outta here," called one outlaw to the others. Slocum shot him. This lent speed to the remaining men's flight. He tried to count them but wasn't sure. There might have been two more. Or three.

Were they among the four who had crossed the original path or did Slocum have them to fight off, too?

"Yee-ha!" shouted one of the freighters. "You done it. You scared them varmints off!"

"Stay down. There might be more," Slocum called. He worried that Abigail would poke her head up again. Her blond hair made a mighty fine target amid the more austere colors worn by the freighters, with their dark hats and filthy shirts.

He made his way back to his skittish horse, mounted and worked his way down the side of the gully, rode past without stopping to see who had been shot, and climbed up the far slope. The outlaw he had shot lay spread-eagle on the ground, the thirsty soil sucking up the blood as it leaked from his body. Slocum didn't find any trace of the other men. He rode a few minutes to the west, thinking he might encounter the four riders on the other road or overtake the ones who had fled.

The Nebraska prairie stretched out as empty as a whore's promise.

Worried that there might be more trouble ahead, Slocum reluctantly returned to the wagons. The drivers had driven up the far gully slope and were ready to finish their trip to No Consequence.

"John, are you all right?" asked Abigail. She hurried to him. "They wanted to press on, but I had to wait for you."

"That was smart. Waiting, that is. I'm all right. And I suspect the road into town from here is safe. That was a mighty big outlaw gang. I killed three and wounded another and don't know how many others there were."

"They're like flies, those road agents," Abigail said bitterly. "We're bringing in so many supplies, they think the pickings will be easy."

"What's the reason you're stocking up the town that much?" he asked.

"We need to impress the men who will issue the bonds. The railroad directors have to be sure No Consequence is the right place for their train station."

"And a prosperous town impresses them better than one on the verge of starvation. This must be costing a pretty penny."

"It's worth it," she assured him. Then the blonde batted her lashes at him and said in a lower voice, "I'll be sure it's worth your while when we get to town. You deserve a reward."

"After I talk to your marshal."

"Always business," Abigail said, sighing. Then she smiled brightly. "That's another thing I like about you!" She turned, whirled her skirts and went back to the buckboard, where she climbed in and gave the order to move out.

Slocum rode from side to side, crossing the trail frequently to be sure they weren't going into another ambush. The road to No Consequence was clear and as safe as an axle-breaking, wheel-cracking dried-mud pair of ruts pretending to be a road could be.

As Slocum rode down the main street, he blinked and wondered if this was a ghost town. It hardly seemed the thriving metropolis Abigail had made it out to be.

The lackluster appearance of the few people poking their heads out to watch the wagons rattle through town told him there weren't as many supporters as Abigail might like.

"There," she called, pointing to the general store. "Unload there."

"Somebody going to inventory the freight as the supplies are put into the store?" asked Slocum.

"No need. I counted everything when it was loaded in North Platte." She saw his quizzical expression. "Oh, it's fine, John. I own the store."

"You do about everything, don't you?" he asked.

"Only with you," she said softly. Then, louder, Abigail called out, "Get the boxes into the store. And will someone find Mr. Petrosian and tell him he's got a customer."

"Who's gonna pay fer the burial?" asked the driver of the lead wagon.

"I will," Abigail said. "Put poor Mr. London into a nice grave. It's the least I can do since he died trying to bring the railroad to No Consequence!"

Slocum caught her excitement again and saw how it affected the townspeople gathering around to see what luxuries Abigail might have brought from North Platte.

"Victor Petrosian is the undertaker," she said to Slocum, as if she needed to talk it out. "I'm so sorry about your friend. When the terminal is built, perhaps we can put a brass plaque up honoring him."

"I reckon it'd have to be put under yours," Slocum said, looking around No Consequence. Whoever had named the town wasn't being funny as much as truthful.

"You're so kind, John. Under that rough exterior, you have a heart of gold."

"Don't tell anyone. With so many road agents out here, they might decide to cut it out."

Abigail started to say something, then bit back the words. She nodded once, as if she had come to a conclusion, then hurried off to speak with a small knot of men, all decked out in Sunday-go-to-meeting clothes.

Slocum supervised the unloading and saw that a good portion of the shipment was fancy cloth for women's clothing and several men's suits. Along with paint, nails and building supplies, they helped Slocum imagine what had been running through Abigail's mind as she had ordered this freight.

She wanted every woman to be gorgeously dressed, every man in a suit, and all the buildings repaired and painted to greet the railroad company directors as they came to town to make their decision.

"That's the lot," the lead teamster said, dusting off his hands. He looked expectantly at Slocum. When Slocum didn't reply, the man cleared his throat. "We need to get paid. I want to hie on back to North Platte for another job since there's not likely any freight going back from here."

"Nothing on the return," mused Slocum. He considered sending Big Ben London back to be buried in North Platte, then figured the man didn't much care what manner of sod dropped on him. Dead was dead. Big Ben had never mentioned family, so getting him put into the ground would end Slocum's responsibility to him.

"Well?" demanded the freighter.

"You'll have to see Miss Stanley. Or the town fathers," Slocum said, looking at the three men who still spoke in guarded tones with her.

"Hate dealin' with a woman, 'specially her," the freighter said. "It's danged hard tellin' 'em you're gonna skin 'em alive if they don't pay up."

Slocum had to laugh. He found it hard to say no to Abigail, also, but for different reasons. Looking around No Consequence convinced him there wasn't anything to keep him here. There were two saloons in the town but neither looked like a hotbed of gambling. Without that the Rockies drew him more powerfully.

He mopped at the sweat on his forehead and went to sit in the shade until Abigail finished her business. Then he could tell her goodbye and head out.

The freighter spoke to her immediately after she turned from the trio. They talked for a moment, then the man heaved a visible sigh of relief when Abigail took him to a gent inside the store, who might have been the town banker from the brief glimpse Slocum got of the man's clothes. The two men vanished into the store, Slocum never getting a good look at the banker. Abigail came to sit beside Slocum in the shade cast by the wall of her store.

"Get the bill settled?" Slocum asked.

"Oh, that. Yes, Mr. Carleton is taking care of it."

"He the town banker?"

"Not much gets by you, does it, John?" She smiled and looked at him. He knew by the woman's expression something more was coming, something he might not find too palatable.

"I know you intend to ride on, but I need a favor. The

railroad directors are coming to town in a few days, and there's a small problem that needs to be resolved."

"You need another carpenter or painter to gussy up the buildings?" Slocum had worked as a carpenter in his day, but the Nebraska heat and the likelihood his merely adequate handiwork wouldn't sway any director to bring the railroad spur to town kept him from volunteering.

"I'm sure we could use one or two, but it's more complicated than that. The road agents are likely gone by now. You put the fear into them," she said.

"There's something else?"

"It might not be anything. Then again, we have to be sure."

"For the railroad directors' sake," Slocum said dryly.

"Yes, yes, exactly, John. I'm so glad you understand why we need to find out if it's true that Sioux have been sighted outside town."

"How many Sioux?"

"We have to find out. And we need to know if they are peaceable." She laid her hand on his and moved a little closer so she could kiss him. "We need to know soon."

Slocum cursed himself as a fool, but he agreed to scout the Indians' camp and report back. So the railroad directors wouldn't be spooked.

5

Slocum couldn't remember when he had been given more supplies for what might be a day or two on the trail. Abigail insisted on outfitting him completely from her store. As he wandered around the large store looking at the goods displayed, he wondered how she intended to sell everything. She carried a huge inventory for a town the size of No Consequence, so much that she had filled a storage shed behind her store as well as stocking the shelves fully. The best Slocum could tell, the only reason No Consequence existed was farming. Wheat and corn fields stretched to the north and east of town. If the railroad came through from the east, a powerful lot of farmers would find themselves with tracks running through their cornfields.

To the south, in the direction of North Platte, Slocum knew there was less than nothing, but if the spur came up from the larger city, No Consequence still held the short straw. Only the crumbs from commerce would land on the plates of the citizens, the best of the money staying in North Platte.

"Anything else, John?" asked Abigail from behind the counter. She brushed a vagrant strand of blond hair from

her eyes. Dust caked her forehead and made her look wild
and free, in stark contrast with her usual focused expression. Slocum wasn't sure which he preferred, since both
were so enticing.

"Got what I need," he said.

"Will that be enough ammunition? Two boxes for your
rifle and plenty of powder, primers and slugs for your six-
gun?"

"If I find more than one or two Sioux warriors, I'm not
going to fight them," he told her. "Count on me hightailing it back. Nobody tangles with the Sioux if they are on
the warpath."

"I suppose not. Caution certainly will gain us more information than shooting it out with the Indians."

Slocum looked at her and wondered if he ought to ask
for a bit more—of something not found on the store's
well-stocked shelves. Then he knew this wasn't the time
or place. Abigail's nerves were frazzled, and he had to
concentrate on not having his scalp lifted by the Sioux.

"I won't be more than a few days," he said.

Abigail opened her mouth, started to say something and
then thought better of it.

"I'll be waiting, John. With luck, the railroad directors
will be here and you can report that there aren't hordes
of Indians ready to scalp any crew laying track across the
prairie."

Slocum nodded, hefted his saddlebags laden with food
and ammo, and went out into the cool evening. He had
considered waiting until the next morning to set out but
had seen how anxious Abigail was to learn what threat
the Sioux posed. The banker had fluttered about like a
bird with a wounded wing but had never said anything,
giving Slocum the feeling that others besides Abigail were
concerned.

He slung his saddlebags over the roan's rump, climbed
into the saddle and headed west. As he rode, leaving No

Consequence far behind, he considered how easy it would be to keep on riding. He had plenty of provisions, thanks to Abigail, with money riding in his pocket after selling the herd in North Platte.

But he owed Abigail the scouting report.

The Big Dipper spun on its handle as he rode, making him wonder how wise it was to blunder around on the prairie in the dark. The sky was moonless, but the Milky Way shone brightly enough to keep his horse from stepping in a prairie dog hole. Slocum drifted as he rode, mulling over everything that had happened. Only when his roan shied did he snap back to alertness.

At first he didn't see or hear anything that might have startled his horse. Then faint cracking sounds reached him. He sniffed deeply and caught the acrid scent of burning buffalo chips. Sound and smell let him find the campsite and the four Sioux sitting huddled around it, blankets pulled up around their shoulders.

Slocum dismounted and made a quick circuit of the Sioux camp, finding no one on guard duty. Four Sioux. From the look of their equipment, this wasn't a war party but a hunting party. A rack of drying meat to one side of the camp completed the picture of peaceful Indians intent on nothing more than feeding their families.

A loud cry caused Slocum to swing around, hand going to the butt of his six-gun. One Sioux threw back his blanket and grabbed a lance.

"Whoa, wait," Slocum cried, moving his hand away from his six-shooter and holding both hands in front of him. "I'm not here to steal your horses."

"Why do you sneak around in our camp?"

By this time, the other three braves had grabbed rifles and knives. Slocum faced four half-asleep, frightened Sioux.

"I came across your camp and thought I saw a wolf sniffing around your game. I chased it off," he said. A wolf howled in the distance, as if agreeing with Slocum's lie. He saw that he could either fight them or soothe their ruffled feathers—and he had no right to be poking around like he was.

Lie, kill or die. There wasn't much choice since Slocum didn't want to shoot it out with men simply hunting.

The four huddled together. Slocum saw they were young, probably out on their first hunt without older braves.

"I'll be going, if that suits you. I don't want any trouble." Slocum kept his hands in plain sight and didn't make any move to leave. He wanted them to agree.

"You no steal?"

"No steal. I am a friend. Will you smoke a pipe?" Slocum reached into his pocket and pulled out a tobacco pouch and let it swing slowly, catching light from the guttering buffalo chip fire.

This settled the matter. Slocum stuffed his tobacco into the Indians' pipe and let them avidly smoke most of it. Then he refilled the pipe, took a puff and passed it along. He guessed the Sioux had been without their ceremonial smoke for some time.

"Are you far from your main camp?" Slocum finally asked after a reasonable time.

"Hunting bad this year. Too dry," one brave said, eagerly taking the pipe from Slocum. "We week's ride from camp. Been gone long."

"You are good hunters," Slocum complimented, "to have so much meat."

The four agreed and began talking of their families, how brave they were in combat—although Slocum doubted any of them had ridden into battle from the lack of scalps at their belts—and of their great hunting prowess. He agreed with them, nodded and finally decided it was time to get back to No Consequence.

"My gift," he said, when he saw the braves eyeing what

remained of the tobacco in his pouch. It was little enough to keep them happy and Abigail could replace the tobacco easily. He remembered the large tins on her store shelves.

The Sioux allowed him to leave without argument. Slocum got onto his tired roan and headed back in the direction of No Consequence, getting a half dozen miles before realizing he had reached the end of his rope and had to rest. He staked out his horse, spread his bedroll and lay down on his back, staring at the stars. Soon enough, his eyelids drooped and he went to sleep dreaming of Abigail and trains and Sioux warriors.

Slocum reined back at the end of No Consequence's main street, feeling uneasy and not knowing why. The Sioux were no threat, and he hadn't seen hide nor hair of the road agents who had killed Big Ben London. They might have run off to lick their wounds, because they weren't likely to bury their dead. The town looked more prosperous to Slocum because some of the paint and supplies Abigail had brought from North Platte had been used to beautify the drab brick buildings. Out here on the plains, wood was in short supply.

If he had had to describe the town as he rode down the street, the only word perfectly fitting No Consequence would have been "idyllic." But something still didn't feel right to him.

Slocum dismounted in front of Abigail's store and went inside, expecting to find a clerk rather than the owner. He was pleasantly surprised to see the blonde busily working behind the counter.

"John! You're back so soon. What did you find?"

He related his night of smoking a pipe with the Sioux and how they were young hunters, not part of a war party. As he spoke he saw the tension melt from her lovely face. She finally came around the counter and clutched him tightly, pressing her face against his chest.

"I'm so relieved to hear this. I don't know what I would have done if the Indians were out scalping people."

"What's the closest army fort?" he asked. "You could have gone there for protection."

"Camp Robinson is the closest," she said, "and it is miles and miles away to the northwest. They could never reach us in time, if there was Indian trouble."

"You could go south to North Platte," he suggested. "Fort Grattan might be closer. Or Fort McPherson." He saw Abigail stiffen with indignation and knew the reason. There was a rivalry—real or perceived by the woman— between North Platte and No Consequence. Going to one of the forts protecting North Platte would be the same as admitting defeat. And if word of it ever got to the railroad directors, they would probably cancel their plans to bring a rail line through Abigail's town.

Abigail's town. That was exactly the way he thought of it, and it seemed all too true. She had everything wrapped up in No Consequence.

"Since the Sioux are pretty much scattered all over the plains, you shouldn't worry about them," he said, trying to soothe her fears.

"Good." Her lips thinned to a line. She looked up at him, her blue eyes beguiling. Abigail relaxed a little and then said, "Please stay, John. I know you were going to ride west. I heard you and Big Ben talking. But stay, for a while longer."

"Until the directors get here?"

"Why not? There's nothing you're riding to. You have no timetable. What're a few days longer?"

"You'd be the only thing keeping me here," Slocum admitted. "I don't hanker to work in corn or wheat fields. From what I saw of the Sioux, the hunting is poor this year, and there's no job in town I'd be willing to fill."

"I know, John. If you stay, it would be as a favor to me."

"Let me think on it," he said. "I've been on the trail too long and need to wet my whistle."

"There are two saloons in town," Abigail said proudly. He contrasted this with how most women acted when drinking whiskey was mentioned. Abigail considered it a mark of progress for No Consequence to have two gin mills. "Gus Gorman runs the Corinthian Palace and his brother Paul owns the Prairie Delight."

"Whichever is closer will do me just fine," Slocum said. He kissed Abigail lightly, tasting her sweet lips. But this wasn't enough to decide him. He left her working on her ledger books and doing a new inventory and stepped outside into the oppressive heat. The Prairie Delight's doors were open and beckoning to him a few yards down the street.

The saloon was larger than he had first expected. Rooms extended off the main room like a rabbit warren, holding games of chance and possibly a crib or two for soiled doves. It bothered him that Abigail would think prostitution was an acceptable part of town, but he decided she either didn't know the Gorman brothers were pimping or he was wrong about what the tiny rooms were actually used for.

"Beer, mister?" asked the barkeep. The man was short, stocky and had huge handlebar mustaches. He twirled the end of one as he shifted from foot to foot behind the bar, as if he were a runner ready for a race and unsure when the starting pistol would sound.

"Whiskey," Slocum said. "Two shots, side by side."

"Coming right up." The barkeep expertly poured the two drinks. Slocum examined one, studying the color and sniffing at it to see how potent it might be. He sampled it, then downed it in a quick gulp. The liquor wasn't as good as he had found in North Platte, but it suited him and his powerful thirst.

"You the fellow who came into town with Miss Abigail?" the barkeep asked.

Slocum nodded.

"Then the drinks are on the house. She's 'bout the best thing that ever happened to this town. She's gonna make us all rich when the railroad comes to town, and any friend of hers is a friend of mine."

"Glad to see folks are so cordial," Slocum said, sipping at his second drink. His tongue and gut weren't deadened enough by the first drink to make this one go down without a bite.

"Yep, No Consequence is going to be the biggest danged town in Nebraska before Miss Abigail is finished with it. She's a real asset to the town."

"Tell me about her," Slocum asked. "Was she born in these parts?"

"Naw, she came from back east. Not sure where, but she's been here going on five years. Her pa and two brothers started the store, but the diphtheria epidemic in '73 took all of them to the Promised Land. Miss Abigail never gave up, though. No, sir."

"That about the time she came up with the idea of bringing the railroad through town?"

"Just about."

Slocum had wondered what put the burr under Abigail's saddle to turn this nothing of a town into a thriving metropolis. He had his answer. Losing her family the way she did made her feel she had to prove herself. Doing what her pa and brothers couldn't would certainly establish her worth, to the town and in her own mind. In a way, Abigail might consider everything she did as a memorial to her family.

By the time Slocum finished his second drink, he had reached his decision. Nothing held him to No Consequence, not even Abigail Stanley. She shared him with her aspirations for the town and wouldn't miss him long when he left. Men came and went but dreams could last forever.

As Slocum stepped outside, he saw a man limping down the street. Slocum started for Abigail's store, then paused. Something about the man struck him as familiar. Then it hit him.

The gimpy man was the one he had shot back in North Platte. He had left him in the town lockup but somehow Rafe Ferguson must have gotten his henchman free.

Slocum swerved, changed direction and cut across the dusty street in time to see the man limp into the town's other saloon. The Corinthian Palace looked like a duplicate of the Prairie Delight. Slocum edged closer, then slipped inside and pressed his back against a cool brick wall so he could view the room.

A door closed at the rear, hinting that the man he had shot had vanished there.

"Howdy," greeted the man behind the bar. Except for the bushy mustaches, he looked like the other barkeep's twin. It didn't take Slocum much to figure they were also the owners, the Gorman brothers.

"What's back there?" asked Slocum, indicating the door where his quarry had disappeared.

"Poker game. But that one's private. If you want, I can ask around and get you into another game."

"Never mind. Give me a beer," Slocum said, dropping a nickel on the bar. He scooped it up, found a table at the far corner of the room and settled down to wait. Sooner or later the limping man had to come out. When he did, Slocum would find out what had brought him to No Consequence.

6

Slocum had hardly drunk half the beer when the limping man came from the side room. Slocum turned slightly in the chair and made certain his six-shooter rode easy, the leather thong free over the hammer. He reached across and rested his hand on the butt of the Colt Navy, then hunkered down and turned away, hiding his face when he saw two more men join the one he had winged back in North Platte.

The one trailing his wounded partner was the man Slocum had kicked in the belly and taken out of the fight. The third man he knew all too well: Rafe Ferguson.

The three men argued among themselves and paid Slocum no attention as they went outside. After they left, Slocum reared back in his chair and craned his neck to peer out the dirty saloon window. The trio stood outside the building arguing. Try as he might, Slocum couldn't hear what they were saying.

"You ready for another beer?" the barkeep called out.

"This one'll do me, thanks," Slocum said, draining the rest of his beer in a single gulp. The three men moved away from the door, and Slocum followed cautiously. He had not expected to see Ferguson again, much less his

two henchmen. Whatever brought them to No Consequence was of interest to Slocum because he figured it
had to do with Abigail Stanley. Maybe Ferguson didn't
like the woman talking the North Platte marshal into letting Slocum go, or maybe it was something else.

If Abigail was right about No Consequence turning into
a boom town when the railroad came in, Ferguson might
have a brand spanking new swindle ready to play on the
citizens.

Slocum had to admit his interest in Ferguson and what
he might be up to had a lot to do with his personal dislike
of the man. Rafe Ferguson was a tinhorn gambler and
cheated whenever he thought he could get by with it. But
the paltry few dollars he had taken from Slocum in a
crooked poker game paled beside siccing his two henchmen on Slocum. That had been uncalled for.

Staying in the shade served the double purpose of keeping Slocum from easy view of the men he followed as
well as preventing the burning sun from sucking out moisture from his body. Ferguson walked with purpose toward
the edge of town where the livery stable stood. If he and
his men rode out of town, Slocum was willing to let them
go.

But they veered from the street and disappeared from
sight. Slocum lengthened his stride and turned the corner
of the bookstore around which Ferguson had vanished.
His hand went to his six-gun and then moved away. A
fourth man had joined Ferguson and his cronies.

They stood in a tight circle, shutting out everyone and
everything else. Slocum's curiosity was getting the better
of him, and he wanted to listen. He stepped back and
looked up the wall of the bookstore. He went back to the
front, jumped and grabbed a drainpipe that creaked and
groaned as it started to come free from its moorings.

Working his feet as much as he could, he drove his toes
into chinks in the mortar between the bricks and got some

traction. Slocum scrambled faster and grabbed the edge of the roof as the drainpipe jerked free. Hanging by his fingers, he began to pull himself up until he could roll onto the edge of the steeply sloping roof.

Slocum wiped sweat from his face, then carefully made his way to the peak of the roof and peered over. The four men still discussed their business, but it looked as if the newcomer was backing off from Ferguson and his partners, trying to distance himself from the swindler.

From the top of the roof, Slocum still couldn't hear. He rolled over the peak and slid down the far side until he caught himself at the back gutter. He was now less than fifteen feet from the men and overheard snippets of what they said.

"We got to this fine town just in time, sir," Ferguson said to the well-dressed man. "You need our services something fierce."

"This isn't right," the man said. He rubbed his palms against his shiny trousers and tried to turn away. Slocum got a better look at him. The man's clothing spoke of money, and the diamond headlight in his silk cravat showed more wealth than Slocum was likely to see in a lifetime. His florid face glistened with sweat as his eyes darted around, looking for a place to run. He was clearly uncomfortable talking with Rafe Ferguson.

That made Slocum think Ferguson was working some sort of swindle and was trying to recruit this prosperous citizen of No Consequence to help him, knowingly or otherwise.

"Right, right, right, what's that mean?" Ferguson asked in his oily tones. "We are men of the world. We see what we want and we seize it!" He grabbed air in front of the man's face. To his credit the man did not recoil. "Don't you see what you want and strive for it? I'm offering you the chance to—"

Slocum felt the shingles under him begin to yield, and

he had to lie back flat on the roof to keep from tumbling off. Gingerly prying the shingles away from his body, he laid them to one side, but by the time he was able to eavesdrop again the details of Ferguson's swindle had been revealed.

"I don't know," the fashion plate said.

"But you'll think on my offer? You won't be disappointed, I promise."

"Yes, I'll consider it all very carefully."

The man turned his back on Ferguson and the others and bustled off, his short legs pumping hard. From what Slocum could tell, the man was a tad on the bowlegged side, hinting at a past spent astride a horse for long hours. If so, he had improved his lot in life. No cowboy sported such fancy duds.

Ferguson and his partners exchanged whispers, cast a look at the man to see if he returned, then the three retraced the route they had taken. Slocum was glad he had clung to the verge of the roof. Otherwise, Ferguson would have spotted him.

Poking his head over the edge of the roof, Slocum saw the well-dressed man go in the back door of a building halfway through town. Gripping the edge of the roof, Slocum swung his long legs over the edge, dangled and then dropped to the ground. He waited a minute to be certain Ferguson didn't return, then went after their mark.

He tried to open the door to follow the man but the door was locked. Slocum went around the building and stepped into the street, staring at the building.

"I'll be damned," he muttered. Then Slocum went into the No Consequence town hall.

"What can I do for you?" asked a clerk behind the counter. The man pushed back half-spectacles on his nose and wiped his ink-spotted hand onto a rag on his desk.

"I'm looking for someone." Slocum described the man he had seen talking to Ferguson.

"That'd be the mayor."

"Would it now?" Slocum nodded knowingly.

"Adam Westfall. He's not in right now. Said he was stepping out to grab a bite to eat. The long hours he spends in his office"—the clerk jerked his thumb over his shoulder in the direction of a closed door at the rear of the room—"don't let him keep a regular schedule."

"I suspect getting the town ready for the railroad directors is keeping him jumping," Slocum said.

"And how. If you want, I can take down your name and arrange an appointment with the mayor sometime later."

"Thanks," Slocum said. "I'll be back. What I had to ask him wasn't that important."

Slocum hesitated in the doorway and caught sight of the mayor's office door opening a crack in a reflection off the inside of the front window. Slocum didn't bother turning to see if the mayor would come out or duck back into his office like a prairie dog diving down its hole when danger neared.

Slocum had promised Abigail he would let her know if he intended riding on right away or if he would stay around town for a spell. Seeing Ferguson with the mayor convinced Slocum he could afford to spend a day or two longer in No Consequence.

He went into Abigail's store as she finished selling a passel of goods to a farmer. The man and his two young sons struggled to get their supplies outside and loaded into their buckboard.

"John, I wasn't sure if I'd see you again."

"I'm like a bad penny. I keep turning up."

"I love it when you're bad," she said, grinning. "Maybe I can close the store for a spell and see just how bad you can be."

Slocum wasn't going to argue with her, but he saw the

expression of lust leave her face to be replaced by one of concern.

"Oh, drat," Abigail said, stamping her foot. "I forgot. The mayor is supposed to give a speech in a few minutes and I can't miss it."

"What's Mayor Westfall talking about?"

Abigail started to speak, then clamped her mouth shut and turned her bright blues eyes fully on Slocum.

"You've been poking around town. I don't remember the mayor's name being mentioned in your hearing. Not while I was around."

"No Consequence is an interesting place," Slocum said noncommittally.

"I don't think Mayor Westfall will talk too long," she said, taking Slocum's arm. "Then we can discuss how long you'll stay. In town, that is."

"If he's like most politicians, he might be talking this time next week, unless the voters start to leave."

"The mayor's a fine speaker. He worked his way up from riding herd in Montana to a position buying horses in North Platte, then he came to town and ran for mayor last year. He's done a splendid job of arranging everything for the railroad."

"Was it his idea or yours?" Slocum asked.

"Mine," Abigail said, no hint of modesty showing. "It didn't take much to convince him and the town council, though. They saw how important a railroad line could be the future of No Consequence."

Arm in arm they walked back to the town hall and went inside. The clerk had abandoned his post and thrown open double doors at the side of the main room, showing a small meeting room with chairs for twenty people and standing room for that many more. Half the seats were already filled.

Abigail hurried in, greeting the people in the front rows and working her way through the crowd. Slocum wondered how long it would be until a town like No Conse-

quence elected a woman as mayor. He knew nothing
about Adam Westfall, but had no doubt that with her skills
Abigail would make a better leader.

The room grew increasingly stuffy as others filed in.
Abigail guided Slocum to a chair at the end of a row near
an open window. The feeble breeze coming in from the
main street helped keep him from sweating like a pig.
They waited only a few minutes more before Adam Westfall made his grand entrance.

Slocum expected to hear a band playing and men carrying flags to precede Westfall. The mayor glad-handed the
men along the aisle as he reached the podium. Reaching
into the inner pocket of his fancy cutaway coat, Westfall
cleared his throat and looked over the crowd.

His eyes locked for an instant with Slocum's, then he
glanced away almost guiltily.

"Ladies and gentlemen, thank you for coming out on
such a fine, hot Nebraska afternoon."

The mayor began droning on with platitudes about how
splendid a town No Consequence was to live in, and Slocum's attention began to drift. He looked out the window,
wondering if he would catch a glimpse of Rafe Ferguson
or his two henchmen. Nothing stirred outside, not even
the dust in the street. It was too hot and still.

And it got hotter inside the town hall as Westfall fell
into the rhythm of his talk. Only when Abigail elbowed
him in the ribs did Slocum snap his attention back to the
mayor.

"I usually don't go on like this, my good friends, but
we have reached the point where this meeting became
imperative. We must join hands and go forth to sell the
municipal bonds necessary for the railroad to come to our
fair town."

A ripple of applause went through the small crowd.

"We have to sell a hundred thousand dollars' worth,"
Abigail whispered. "It is going to be difficult, but without

the money, there's no way we can attract the railroad."

Slocum's eyebrows rose at the amount.

"What does the railroad company need with the money?" he asked suspiciously. "Is it a bribe?"

"Not at all!" Abigail said. She settled down and half turned toward Slocum. "It is development money. We cannot expect the railroad to bear the entire financial burden. With a stake in the line, everyone in town is more likely to pull together."

Abigail fell silent as Mayor Westfall began explaining how they all needed to sell bonds to their neighbors, to friends, to anyone with a few dollars willing to invest.

"And what an investment in our future it will be!" he cried. "The plains will blossom with our agriculture and herds, all destined for markets back east. The access the railroad will afford No Consequence is beyond price. And," Westfall said, his voice dropping to capture the crowd's attention fully, "we can all benefit, if we own the bonds ourselves."

"How's that possible?" asked a skeptical farmer on the other side of the room.

"If you invest one hundred dollars, you will receive back one hundred fifty in only five years. The hundred dollars now will go to the railroad; taxes will pay back the interest."

"Since I have to pay taxes, that sorta sounds like I'd be payin' myself. That don't make sense."

A ripple of agreement spread through the room.

"You won't be paying that much in taxes," Westfall said. "No Consequence will become a center for commerce. Taxes paid by those dealing with us will more than repay the debt. The money both to develop and to pay back the bonds will come from outside No Consequence."

"But we have to put up that hundred dollars to start?" asked the farmer.

"Yes, and you will be rewarded many times over—in money, in new markets, in prosperity!"

"Well, if I don't have to pay the taxes that'll pay off the bonds, sign me up for five hundred dollars!" The farmer jumped to his feet and began fumbling for a wad of greenbacks in his pocket.

The others in the room were slower to line up to pledge their money, but Slocum saw the rock beginning to roll downhill. He wasn't sure it could be stopped—or if anyone should try.

7

"Why should I go along?" Slocum asked. He stood just inside the door of Abigail's store, staring out into the already hot Nebraska day. After the mayor had made his call for every citizen of No Consequence to buy—and to sell to their neighbors—the bonds necessary for bringing the railroad to town, Slocum and Abigail had returned to her store and the small living quarters behind it. The night had passed pleasurably but much too fast.

The sun poked its red disk above the eastern horizon and began the constant chore of burning everything under it far too soon for Slocum's liking. The idea of venturing out onto the prairie with the mayor and a gaggle of farmers in tow struck him as ridiculous.

"You don't have to, John. You don't have to do anything you don't want," Abigail said. "But I'm going. Mayor Westfall needs all the help he can get to persuade the surrounding farmers of their part in the town's progress. If you came with us, you could see something of the good people here and know how vital it is to them for the railroad spur to be built."

"Doesn't much matter to me what's good or not for No Consequence," Slocum allowed. "You live here. You ought to decide for yourself. Each and every one of you."

"But this is *important*, John," Abigail said earnestly. The blonde pushed her bangs back from her forehead and sucked in a lungful of air that caused her breasts to rise and fall enough to catch his attention. Clothed or bare, those were mighty fine womanly attributes.

"Besides you and the mayor, who's going?"

"A half dozen farmers, all backers of the project. We have to meet with others who aren't as dedicated."

"You mean you have to argue with farmers who don't want any part of the rails crossing their property."

"That's what part of the hundred thousand dollars is for, John. We need to buy right-of-way across many of the farmers' fields. But they will benefit. They—"

"You don't have to convince me," he said. "I'll ride along."

"You make it sound as if you want to watch for something," Abigail said.

"I don't have any trouble admitting that," Slocum said, grinning. "You're the one I want to watch."

Abigail laughed. "You're incorrigible. Let's get saddled and join the mayor and the farmers who'll go with us. They're assembling in front of town hall in a few minutes."

"Are you riding or taking your buckboard?" Slocum asked.

"Riding." Abigail batted her eyelashes at him and added, "If you're lucky, you might catch a glimpse of my legs."

"Count me in," Slocum said. He wanted to see who else went with the mayor. If Rafe Ferguson rode with the politician, something was rotten at the town hall.

There might be something rotten even if Ferguson didn't join Adam Westfall on this trip. Ferguson and his cronies hadn't buttonholed the mayor for no reason.

Slocum saddled Abigail's horse, a paint mare, and then

got the saddle onto his more powerful roan. They rode slowly from the small stable behind Abigail's store next to her storage shed and around to the town hall. The mayor sat in his carriage, haranguing two farmers.

"You'll benefit fourteen ways to Sunday, David. You'll earn interest on the bond you buy, the town'll give you money for right-of-way across land that's not doing you much good anyhow, then when the railroad is finished building, you can sell your wheat in a bigger market back east. There's no way you can lose if you invest a few dollars now."

"You're asking for 'bout all the money me and the missus have saved up, Mayor," the farmer said. He scratched himself, looked as if he was passing a stone and then said, "I reckon you're right. Put me down for two hundred dollars' worth of them munny-nissi-pul bonds."

"Excellent, David, excellent. You have made a decision that is the turning point of your life. Before, you were poor. Now you will prosper."

"Hope that's right, Mayor. It surely has been hard growing in this heat and drought. I can do with some good luck."

"It won't be luck, David. It'll be your wisdom that makes you a wealthy farmer."

"You're handin' him a bill of goods, Westfall," the other farmer said. "We kin use wagons and git our grain to North Platte."

"Over vast stretches of desolate prairie fraught with immense dangers," Mayor Westfall said smoothly. Slocum was fascinated with how easily the politician met the objections of his constituents. "It's a hard three- or four-day trip, if the weather is agreeable. There are Sioux Indians on the warpath all the time, and road agents! Why those brigands seek to choke off our current trade route with North Platte!"

"I kin shoot straight. And what outlaw wants a wagonload of grain?"

"I forgot the worst danger of all," Adam Westfall went on, as if he didn't hear the farmer. "North Platte grain dealers! They are completely unrepentant crooks. They know they can force you to sell for next to nothing, then ship your grain on their railroad and get top dollar for it. We have no other market."

"Unless the railroad is built," Abigail chimed in, her cheeks flushed with excitement. "You can't deny how important it is to have more than the one market, besides North Platte," she said. "With a train loaded with your grain heading to the markets along the Mississippi, why, you might get twice what anyone in North Platte would buy for."

"Twice? I have to disagree, Miss Abigail," Westfall said. "I think everyone could see a dozen times the going rate in North Platte."

This caused a buzz among the small crowd that had gathered, but the second farmer still wasn't convinced.

Slocum couldn't fault the mayor's logic, especially when it came to how merchants in North Platte would try to cheat anyone from No Consequence selling their crops. He started to ask about Rafe Ferguson, but the mayor held up his hand, stood in his carriage and waved his arms to get everyone's attention.

"We need to get on the road. We have bonds to sell and a railroad to build! Come along, David. You, too, Frederick." The mayor beckoned to the reluctant farmer. "A few hours of your time is all I ask. You owe it to the town since your farm is vital to the railroad."

"You goin' to see the others? I don't think I want any part of this, but if the rest go along, I'll reconsider."

"Excellent, Frederick, excellent. Do what is best for you but consider the others in our community." Frederick jumped up and settled beside the mayor, with David on the far side. They started arguing over rights-of-way and cost immediately.

The mayor snapped the reins and got his horse pulling the light carriage. The politician rattled off, letting the rest of his retinue fall in line behind him.

Slocum kept an eagle eye out as he rode from town, looking for any trace of Ferguson or his henchmen. They had made themselves scarce since he had seen them with the mayor the day before. Slocum didn't know if that was good or if it ought to worry him.

The two reluctant farmers rode with the mayor. From the way they warmed up, Slocum reckoned the mayor had won them both over to buying the town's bonds.

"How much are you investing in the bonds?" Slocum asked Abigail suddenly. The thought hadn't occurred to him before, but the woman was such a staunch supporter, he thought she must be heavily invested.

"I've put in as much as I can," she said. "I owe a great deal to my suppliers in North Platte. But I'll turn a quick profit on all the merchandise because the railroad crews will need to eat. Until they get a line built, they won't be able to bring in their supplies, so they must buy from me."

"The bonds," Slocum urged.

"All I had left was, well, my parents' legacy. I'm putting a second mortgage on the store and investing that in the bonds. Almost ten thousand dollars."

Slocum blinked in surprise. Abigail alone was purchasing ten percent of the total bond obligation.

"I intend for No Consequence to prosper, and I'll be prospering with it," she said firmly.

"Hold on," Slocum said, sitting straighter in the saddle. "I see a powerful lot of dust being kicked up ahead. There might be trouble brewing."

"No, no, John, there isn't. A couple men who support the mayor rounded up some of the farmers who don't want to invest. This way we can talk to them outside town, so there's not as much pressure on them. Besides, many can't take the time to go to town and leave their farms."

Slocum rode ahead and saw Abigail was right. A dozen farmers, crowded into a big tent with flapping canvas sides, tried to stay away from the sizzling sun the best they could. Since it was well past noon, any bit of shadow was appreciated. One farmer passed around a jug filled with corn squeezings. Slocum couldn't tell if he supported the mayor or if he was only here to get drunk.

"You with the mayor?" called the farmer with the jug. "Where is that varmint? We got work to do, and he promised us some food and liquor."

"I don't know about that," Slocum said, "but the mayor's on his way in a carriage. That's going to take him a few minutes longer." He turned in the saddle and saw Abigail riding up fast. From her expression something was wrong.

"John, John!" she cried. "Road agents! They're attacking the mayor!"

This caused a furor among the gathered farmers. Slocum saw that none of the men were armed.

"Stay put," Slocum said. He wheeled his stallion around and galloped back along the road, flashing past Abigail. He spotted the mayor with the two farmers riding alongside him in the carriage, trying to avoid three masked men who fired wildly at them.

The mayor went off the road and a wheel hit a rock, spinning the light carriage around. Then it toppled over, sending the three men inside flying. The frightened horse reared; pawed at the air, then snapped its bridle and raced away.

Slocum cleared leather and began flinging lead in the direction of the three outlaws. His sudden arrival threw them into confusion and they milled around, unsure what to do. Then their leader fired several times in Slocum's direction. One slug whined past Slocum's ear, but this was the full extent of the threat posed by the outlaws' poor marksmanship. They seemed to understand their easy robbery had turned dangerous for them and turned tail.

"No, Mr. Slocum, wait!" shouted the mayor. "Don't go after them. Three against one. You'd get hurt."

Slocum reined in and stared at the mayor. The politician's clothing was torn and dirty but otherwise he was in one piece. The two farmers picked themselves up and brushed off the dirt, none the worse for wear.

"You know, David," drawled one, "I never did like them carriages. Always preferred sturdier wagons."

They laughed and Slocum knew they weren't injured, either.

"Help us get the carriage upright. And can you fetch my horse?" asked the mayor. Slocum trotted after the frightened horse and found it less than a quarter mile off. It had been spooked, run itself out and then tried to find some decent grass to munch on. He led the horse back. The mayor and his two helpers had the carriage back on its wheels and pushed onto the road.

It took a few minutes to get the horse hitched. Then Adam Westfall chattered like a magpie the entire time it took to reach the tent filled with farmers.

"You get yerself shot up, Mayor?" asked a farmer.

"By the grace of God and Mr. Slocum's quick rescue, no," Westfall said. "But this sort of thing is going to happen more and more," the mayor said.

"What're you sayin'?"

"The more prosperous No Consequence gets, the more we will attract such lowlifes," Westfall said. "We will grow more, sell more, be worth more. But this won't happen if there is a train serving our fine community. You will be able to send your crops east quickly and receive payment as easily, thanks to the marvel of the iron horse!"

Slocum drew back and let the mayor make his sales

pitch about the railroad, the bonds, the prosperity and safety waiting for the citizens in and around No Consequence. The words fell on his deaf ears because he had recognized the road agents attacking the mayor and the two farmers now converted to the mayor's way of thinking.

Rafe Ferguson and his partners weren't any better robbers than they were crooked gamblers.

8

"A most successful day, yes, it was," chortled Adam
Westfall, rubbing his hands together. He came closer to
Slocum and thrust out his hand. "I want to thank you for
saving me and the two fine farmers on the road to the
confab," he said. The mayor smiled so broadly Slocum
wondered if the man intended to grab him in a bear hug.

To keep that from happening, Slocum shook the politician's hand and said, "It wasn't anything."

"You're too modest. Why, every wagon train in the
area has been beset by road agents. Who would have
thought they would have tried to rob me on my way to
discuss the very thing that will stop their felonious activ-
ities?"

"Why can't they rob a train as easily as they do a
wagon train?" asked Slocum. "If anything, they have more
passengers to rob and the mail car usually has a safe filled
with money on its way somewhere."

Westfall cleared his throat, harrumphed loudly and
turned from Slocum, speaking to the crowd on the steps
of the town hall.

"Yes, Mr. Slocum saved the day this time, but how long
will we have such a heroic figure in our fair town? We

need to discuss how quickly we can sell our bonds to start the railroad!"

A cheer went up from the small crowd, who followed Westfall into the town hall to discuss the sales venture. Slocum brushed the dust off his clothing and watched what he thought was a big swindle, with Rafe Ferguson in the middle of it somehow.

"You were so brave today, John. Thank you for saving the mayor and those two farmers from what would have been a terrible theft." Abigail's blue eyes shone with admiration, but Slocum turned away from it. He hadn't been the least bit brave—and there hadn't been any danger.

"I doubt it," he said dryly. Abigail looked at him strangely and started to ask what he meant, but he cut her off. "Do you know a man name Ferguson?"

"Is he a farmer? I know everyone within a hundred miles of town, but unless you mean Fogel, or perhaps Frederick Healey—he was with the mayor today—I don't think so."

"He's a tinhorn gambler and has two henchmen with him. One limps and the other's got a boot print in his belly."

"John, have you been out in the sun too long?" Abigail looked concerned.

"No," he said. "I need to get some food and then I'll be riding on."

"Oh," she said in a small voice. Her disappointment was clear on her pretty face.

"I'll be back in a week or so. I need some information about the spur line that'll come into town."

"Do you know someone who might want to invest in the bonds?" Her eagerness now knew no bounds.

"Could be. Which rail line is thinking about coming over from Omaha?"

"The Platte and Central Plains," she said, hooking her arm in his. They started toward the small restaurant a few doors down from her store. Abigail bent his ear for more than an hour with every possible detail of the transaction, how the railroad would be funded and the men responsible for it on the Platte & Central Plains end in Omaha. Slocum shoveled food in, chewed mechanically, drank coffee and listened. Eventually Abigail started repeating herself, and he knew it was time to go.

"You keep a sharp eye out for Rafe Ferguson and the men I told you about," Slocum said. "If you see them, tell the marshal." He hesitated, then asked, "No Consequence does have a marshal, doesn't it?"

"Not exactly," she said. "The Thomas County sheriff or one of his deputies comes over from Seneca—that's the county seat—if there's any trouble. This is a peaceable town and we never have any trouble. Or not much," she said.

"The railroad will bring in more folks, and you'll need a full-time marshal," Slocum said.

"About six feet tall, with green eyes and ever so handsome and talented?" Abigail said, running her fingers over Slocum's shirt.

"I'm not lawman material," he said. "See you in a week or so." With that Slocum mounted and started on the trail east to Omaha.

Omaha was larger than Slocum liked. Too many people crowding around, but something of the energy and enthusiasm of the city kept him fired up because it reminded him of Abigail Stanley. He had ridden hard for three days to reach the city and now he had to find the offices of the Platte & Central Plains Railroad. It proved harder than he had thought.

He tied up his horse and went into the Central Pacific offices near the large rail yards north of the city. Inside, a dozen clerks labored over ledgers. It took him a few minutes to attract the attention of one. The man blinked at Slocum, then came over.

"Passenger tickets are sold over at the depot. We don't do anything but freight shipping here," the man said in way of greeting.

"I'm not looking to buy a ticket," Slocum said. "I got a mite turned around. I was given directions to the Platte and Central Plains office but can't seem to remember how to find it."

The clerk scowled and shook his head.

"Never heard of it. What is it?"

"A railroad," Slocum said. "The Platte and Central Plains Railroad. They're planning a spur line through central Nebraska over to No Consequence."

"No Consequence? Never heard of it. Never heard of any Platte and Central Plains, either. I've got to get back to work. If you need freight rates, I can supply that. But nothing more."

"What other railroads run west from here across Nebraska?"

"Our competitors," the clerk said snippily. Slocum knew he wasn't going to find out any more information.

He began poking around, looking at the names painted on the sides of the freight cars in the yards and trying to find someone—anyone—who could direct him to the Platte & Central Plains offices. He finally found a down-on-his-luck man sitting in the shade some distance from the yards who beckoned Slocum over.

"I heard you askin' 'bout railroads. There's not much 'bout 'em I don't know."

"You a rail worker?" Slocum asked, sitting beside the man.

"Used to be. Got my leg crushed when some steel rail fell off a flatbed. Been hangin' around, tryin' to find somethin' to do ever since."

The man passed Slocum a whiskey bottle with a finger

of amber fluid left in it. Slocum took a pull, then handed it back.

"That's mighty potent whiskey. Goes down smooth, though."

"Got it off a conductor who made a swing through Kentucky. He owed me."

"Thanks for letting me take a swig," Slocum said.

"What are you askin' about? Saw how you came out of the CP office. Buncha sonsabitches there. I know 'em all."

"I ruffled their feathers asking which roads run west," Slocum said. "Some folks don't like talking about their competition."

"No competition to the CP, dang it," the man said.

"What about the Platte and Central Plains?"

"Never heard of it. Then again, lots of tiny little itty-bitty roads crop up all the time. Run a few miles of track, then go out of business. Where they from?"

"Omaha. Going to a small town named No Consequence smack in the middle of Nebraska."

"Ain't runnin' the line from here. Nobody's buildin' track right now. The Panic of '73 put most of the smaller lines out of business and scared the big ones like the CP."

Slocum thought about this awhile as he watched the trains rattle and clank out, smelled the coal smoke from their boilers and batted at hot cinders trying to burn his skin.

"No doubt that there isn't a Platte and Central Plains Railroad?" he finally asked. Slocum watched the man's reaction carefully.

"There's always some doubt, but I ain't heard of it. And I listen good. I want a job. Don't care if it is railroad detective or conductor. Just 'cuz I got a game leg don't mean I can't work and use my head."

"Much obliged," Slocum said.

"If you find this here Platte and Central Plains and they

need experienced help, you look me up. Name's Will Mason."

"That I will, Mr. Mason. Thanks."

Slocum mounted and rode back into Omaha, having not given up on finding the company Adam Westfall and Abigail and the others in No Consequence were placing so much faith in for the revitalization of their town. But a full day's asking around produced nothing more than Will Mason had told him. As Slocum rode back by the railroad yards, he saw the man sitting where he had left him the day before.

"Mason!" he called.

"You find them varmints that are puttin' in a road to the middle of nothing?" Mason called.

"Nope, but I figured you could use this while we're both looking," Slocum said. He fished around in his saddlebags and pulled out a bottle of whiskey, the best he could find in Omaha. "Don't reckon it's up to that you shared with me, but it might keep you going until you find that job."

"Much obliged," Mason said, popping the cork and taking an appreciative drink. Mason held it up for Slocum to sample but he shook his head.

"Don't want to fall off my horse in the middle of the prairie," Slocum said.

"You might get runned over by the Platte and Central Plains laying tracks," said Mason, laughing. "See you around."

Slocum touched the brim of his Stetson and turned his stallion's face toward the west. He knew how long and hot the ride was, and he was going back to give Abigail some bad news.

It was getting toward twilight of the seventh day he had been gone from No Consequence when Slocum rode back into town. The first time he had come, No Consequence looked like a ghost town. No longer. People hurried up and down the street, doing what they could to gussy up the appearance of the brick buildings. For the sod houses and other quarters, there wasn't a lot they could do except drape red, white and blue crepe banners across them. But everyone had caught the railroad fever that already infected Abigail Stanley.

Slocum looked at the woman's store and saw a kerosene light burning inside. She worked late, as did most of the people. He considered riding directly to her store and telling her what he had discovered in Omaha, but a better idea came to him:

Go right to the source of the infection and cut it out.

Slocum dismounted in front of the town hall and went inside. The clerk had long since left, but the door to the mayor's office stood open. Laboring over a stack of papers, Adam Westfall never saw or heard Slocum until he rapped on the door. The politician jumped as if someone had stuck him with a pin.

"Mr. Slocum, come in. I hadn't seen you around for a spell and thought you'd left our fair town. Pull up a chair and take a load off."

"I got a load of something to talk about, Mayor, but a chair's not going to be strong enough."

"What are you going on about?" Westfall leaned back in his chair and laced his fingers behind his head. Sitting this way caused his paunch to become more prominent, but the mayor didn't seem to mind or even much notice. "I got plenty of important work to do, so don't waste my time. The directors are coming soon, and I want everything in town shipshape and ready to impress them."

"There isn't a Platte and Central Plains Railroad," Slocum said flatly.

"I, uh, what are you telling me, Slocum? Of course there is. The directors are due into No Consequence within the week."

"I spent a considerable amount of time trying to find anyone in Omaha who knew anything about the Platte and Central Plains or any other railroad building a spur line in this direction. The companies that didn't go belly up aren't expanding. There isn't a railroad coming to town."

"I, well, that is," sputtered Westfall. Then he rocked forward, looked around as if he was ready to share a deep, dark secret with Slocum, and said, "This is a highly confidential matter, Mr. Slocum. The very financial troubles you alluded to are the reason the directors wanted to keep the spur line quiet from their competitors. A hundred-thousand-dollar grant from anywhere is mighty enticing to a company right now."

"You're saying there is a Platte and Central Plains and the men who run it are keeping it a secret?" Slocum didn't know whether to laugh or reach across the desk and shake the truth out of Westfall.

"Not exactly. There isn't a railroad named the Platte and Central Plains. There will be, when the spur line is built into town. Right now, this is a secret project of the Northern Pacific Railroad, the CP's biggest competitor. The Northern is looking for a way across the country farther south than their regular line. They want to use No Consequence as a depot, a major switching yard, but they dare not let on to the CP. Railroad wars get mighty vicious, and exposing my citizens to that would be sheer folly."

"Folly," Slocum repeated, still considering if throttling Westfall would get the truth out.

"The other companies would muscle in on the NP— what I shall continue to call the Platte and Central Plains, since that will soon be the name of their subsidiary line. We stand to profit from the arrival of such a major force in railroading. Don't upset the apple cart, Mr. Slocum, by spreading rumors about it. I beg you."

Slocum thought hard and fast. What Adam Westfall

said might be true, but there wasn't the ring of authenticity to it Slocum wanted. It sounded more like a lie thought up to tell if someone, like Slocum, twigged to the fraud being perpetrated on the town.

"There's more," Slocum said. "When you and the farmers were held up on the road—"

"Ah, yes, such bravery you showed! You are a true hero and—"

"And nothing," snapped Slocum. "You had Abigail ask me along because you knew you were going to be held up and that I'd scare off the so-called road agents."

"So-called! Why, they ply their trade all around No Consequence!"

"Rafe Ferguson, you mean? And his two henchmen?" Slocum saw the color drain from Westfall's face.

"Please, Slocum, I admit it. I set up the robbery. I hired Ferguson and his friends to pretend to be outlaws to impress the point on the farmers. It was dishonest, I know, but it worked. They all agreed to buy bonds. There have been road agents in the area, but I couldn't rely on them trying to hold me up. And if real ones had, people might have been hurt."

"Ferguson is a crooked gambler and a swindler," Slocum said. Realizing it had been Rafe Ferguson posing as an outlaw had set Slocum on the road to Omaha to check on the details of the railroad construction.

"I had no idea. He and his two friends came to town, and since they weren't known, I approached them with my little stunt. That's all it was, Mr. Slocum. Believe me. I have only the best interest of the community at heart."

As sincere as Westfall sounded, Slocum still wasn't buying it. But he knew Abigail would. She wanted to believe the railroad was coming to make them all rich and to put "her" town on the map. It was as much a tribute to her deceased family as it was a key to financial prosperity for her.

"I need to think over what you've told me," Slocum said. "I still don't buy it, but what you say might be true."

"It is, Mr. Slocum. The Gospel truth!"

Slocum left the mayor's office and stepped into the humid Nebraska evening. How it could be so dry and yet have the air feel so sticky with moisture was something he didn't want to think about. But he had to decide what to tell Abigail. Slocum headed for the Corinthian Palace and saw one of the Gorman brothers behind the bar. He ordered a single shot to cut the trail dust and give him a few minutes to think.

The whiskey was nowhere near as good as that given him by Will Mason. Slocum finished the drink and left, going back into the street, now as dark as the inside of a shroud.

He was headed for Abigail's store when the shot rang out. Slocum felt the bullet whiz by as he dove face forward into the dust.

9

Slocum lay unmoving in the dust, waiting for something to happen. He doubted a second bullet would be fired unless he stirred, and he hoped the bushwhacker would mosey out from hiding to see how well the first shot had done its job.

Blinking dirt from his eyes, he peered along the street and saw a few curious souls venturing out to see what had caused the ruckus. Slocum realized the back-shooting son of a bitch who had tried to gun him down wasn't going to show himself now, and if he did, Slocum might not be able to separate him from the rest of the crowd.

Rolling fast, he feinted left in case the sniper watched him, then reversed and rolled right, coming to a sitting position so he could get out his six-shooter. No second shot came to rob him of life. He looked behind him but couldn't pinpoint where the shooter had been.

"You all right, Mr. Slocum?" asked a man who had staggered from the saloon. He was mostly drunk and still held a beer glass in his hand. "What happened? Too much to drink?"

"I'm all right," Slocum said, getting to his feet. His hand began to cramp from his grip on the Colt Navy, ready to return fire at any instant. But as he scanned the puzzled crowd he saw no one looking angry at having missed an easy shot. Looking higher, he thought he saw a perfect spot on a two-story building next to the saloon where a gunman might have fired.

"What's going on?" came Adam Westfall's irked question. "We can't all loaf around lollygagging when there's work to be done. The directors will be here too soon for anyone to slacken now."

Slocum glared at the mayor, who refused to meet his gaze. That told Slocum all he needed to know. Westfall hadn't pulled the trigger, but he had told someone everything Slocum had revealed earlier about his trip to Omaha. If Slocum were to put money to bet, he'd have given even odds on that person being Rafe Ferguson.

Slocum had intended leaving No Consequence but couldn't because of the shooting. He had a score to settle, both for himself and for Big Ben London. He pushed through the crowd, turning his back to Abigail's store. If Westfall had done nothing, Slocum would have told the lovely blonde what he had discovered, she would probably not have believed a word of it, and he would have left town.

Not now.

After he found Rafe Ferguson and his two partners, he would decide what to do about the mayor. Slocum pushed through the crowd and went to the building where the sniper most likely had taken his shot. The two-story structure held a dress shop, the owner apparently living on the second floor. Slocum rushed past the startled women inside, then stopped at the stairs leading up.

"Has anyone come down in the past couple minutes?" he asked the clerk behind the counter. She was measuring off a few yards of inexpensive gingham for someone, her customer plainly from a nearby farm by the look of her clothing.

"I heard something out back."

"Before or after the gunshot?"

"After, but—"

She spoke to empty air. Slocum found the rear door and burst through it. He found where a horse had been tethered long enough to leave a pile of manure behind. Fresh, so fresh the flies hadn't found it yet. From the hoofprints in the dry dirt, the bushwhacker had headed north out of town. Slocum stepped back and saw scrapes and scuffs on the brick and a tall lightning rod, bent half over, on the roof. A rope tied around that lightning rod would have afforded a man quick descent and an even quicker escape after he missed.

Or did he think he had succeeded in killing Slocum?

He hadn't had time to see Slocum was only playing possum. And the mayor had been surprised to find Slocum still alive and kicking. That meant the mayor might contact Rafe Ferguson as soon as he could—but right now Ferguson and his confederates thought Slocum was a goner.

Slocum wasted no time getting his stallion and finding the trail north. He doubted Ferguson camped too far outside No Consequence, because he needed to be in touch with Adam Westfall to find out who and what to stick up to make the farmers think travel in the area was less dangerous via rail. Slocum had to hand it to the mayor. It was a fine line to walk. If Ferguson got too frisky and shot up a supply wagon or robbed too many farmers, they would get the sheriff from Seneca to stop him—or worse, organize a vigilance committee. That would detract from the plan to get the Platte & Central Plains Railroad into town.

And to sell the bonds to entice the nonexistent railroad to build here. Slocum had heard the mayor's reasons why he had not found the Platte & Central Plains office in Omaha and had not believed a word of it.

Slocum was a good tracker, but the hoofprints became harder and harder to follow until he gave up hunting for them in the dry dust and grass and relied on the rider keeping to a straight path across the prairie. When he topped a rise and looked over a broad, shallow basin of gently swaying grass, Slocum caught sight of his quarry almost two miles off.

He urged his stallion to a trot and kept the pace as long as he could, closing the gap until the man suddenly vanished from sight. Slocum worried the bushwhacker might be laying a new trap for him and left his beeline to circle about. The extra time Slocum spent going around like that gave his quarry time to vanish into thin air.

It was getting late in the day, but Slocum refused to give up. He searched fruitlessly until twilight turned to darkness and prevented him from ever finding a trail across the plains. Reluctant to give up but realizing he had no choice, Slocum found some buffalo chips, made a sputtering fire and pitched camp.

He ate a quick meal from provisions in his saddlebags, then hiked to the top of a low hill and looked over the prairie, hoping to catch sight of another camp fire. No matter where he looked or how hard he sniffed the humid night air for smoke, he found nothing.

Disgusted with his turn of bad luck, Slocum went back to his camp and put out the fire. If he could hunt for Ferguson's fire, Ferguson could look for his, although Slocum had no idea if the swindler even knew he was being chased. The bushwhacker—and Slocum knew he was making a big assumption that the man he had sighted even was his would-be killer—might have gone to ground for other reasons. He might not have seen Slocum at all.

Slocum lay back, staring into the starry night sky and fuming at the way things were turning out. Catching Ferguson and questioning him would provide evidence even Abigail could not deny that the mayor was up to no good.

Even more, capturing the man who had tried to back-shoot him would take a weight off Slocum's mind. He wanted to get even. And when he evened the score, the bushwhacker wasn't likely to try killing anyone else.

Ever again.

As Slocum stared up into the heavens, clouds began drifting in from the west. The way they billowed and surged, blocking more of the sky with every passing minute, Slocum knew he might be in for a real downpour. If that happened, the prairie would turn to a swamp and any tracks left by the bushwhacker would be obliterated. But that wouldn't stop him. He knew Ferguson and his gang were out here somewhere.

Slocum fell into a troubled sleep filled with gunshots and train whistles and Adam Westfall laughing at him.

The fitful rain was hardly enough to blot out the trail, but Slocum still hadn't found the tracks he so diligently sought. Sweeping in a wide arc back and forth over the area where the rider had disappeared from sight the day before availed him little. He found a few yards of double ruts left by wagon wheels. Possibly a small wagon train from the look of it, but after a short distance they vanished, telling him how long ago the wheels had passed this way.

Sporadic fat drops of tepid rain spattered against his hands and face, forcing him to get out his slicker. Stubbornly, he refused to give up the hunt, but increasingly he saw how futile it was. He hunkered down and went to the top of one of the rolling hills to study the land. The prairie grasses had perked up, even with the hint of rain that had fallen since the prior night, but nowhere did he see a trace of the man—the gang—he sought.

Slocum got his bearings, looked both east and west in case Ferguson might have a camp down in one of the deep ravines, and then rode north, figuring the rider from the day before might have taken a detour and then returned to his steadfast route.

Rain began coming down harder and harder, but Slocum rode on until he reached an old abandoned farm. His heart jumped in his chest. On the lee side grazed a small horse obviously broken for riding and not plowing. Whoever had ridden the horse had taken off the saddle and was probably inside the sod hut. No smoke came curling out of the chimney, nor was there any light shining out the partially opened door.

From the look of the door, it wouldn't close because it was almost off its hinges. The other signs of neglect told Slocum the farm had been deserted for at least a year. The drought might have driven the farmer and his family to some other, more prosperous spot, or they could have given up and gone into No Consequence.

They might have even died and been buried somewhere around the sod house. Disease was a constant menace out on the prairie.

But the menace Slocum faced now wasn't cholera. It carried a six-shooter and had tried to bushwhack him.

He dismounted some distance from the house and advanced, the rain hammering more fiercely at him now. His roan gratefully pushed aside the smaller mare to get into the dubious shelter offered by the wall of the sod house. Slocum slipped his six-gun from his holster and walked softly to the door.

Rain pounded down now loud enough to cover any small noises he might make. From inside he heard sounds of someone moving around, humming and busily fixing a cold noontime meal.

Slocum tried the door and saw it wouldn't move. Dust had blown up around the base, gotten wet and then dried into rock-hard mud. He had only a small space to squeeze through. Cocking his six-shooter, he braced himself, then burst through the gap into the dark interior of the sod house.

"Hands up!" he cried, expecting to shoot the instant his quarry went for a six-gun. A surprised feminine squeal met his demand. As his eyes adjusted to the dim interior he saw Abigail Stanley with her hands high. She was naked to the waist.

"John! I—What's going on?"

He lowered the hammer on his six-shooter and slipped it back into the cross-draw holster.

"Sorry. I thought you were the bushwhacker I've been tracking."

"Well, I'm not," she said indignantly. Abigail looked down and seemed to notice for the first time she was partially exposed to his lustful gaze.

"Do you always travel like that?" he asked.

"Only when I get my blouse wet from the rain. I didn't think to bring a slicker." She crossed her arms over her breasts to hide them from him. Then Abigail lowered them so the twin globes of snowy white flesh jostled about gently.

"What are you staring at?" she demanded.

"About the prettiest sight I ever saw on the prairie," Slocum said. He came in and looked around the single-room sod hut. His guess had been right. Whoever had lived here had moved on a spell back. All the cooking gear was gone, including the iron stove, which explained why there wasn't any smoke coming out the chimney. If Abigail had started a fire, it would have filled the room with smoke in nothing flat.

"I'm not staying too long," Abigail said. "Only until the rain's over."

"Why are you out here? Not to get a bath," Slocum said.

"A bath," Abigail mused. "What a wonderful idea. I find the interior of this sod house so depressingly filthy."

She looked up as water dripped down through the dried roof. It would stop in a little while when the dirt turned to mud and sealed the crevices between hunks of sod.

"What do you mean?" Slocum unslung his gun belt and tossed his hat aside, ready to continue stripping down. The bed didn't look too inviting but Abigail had brought in her saddle and blanket. That might be good enough for what he had in mind.

But it wasn't what the seductive blond filly wanted.

She skinned out of her riding skirts and kicked them aside, then picked them up and carefully dangled them from a peg to keep them from getting any dirtier on the floor. Abigail wore only bloomers. She looked back over her shoulder coyly, an impish grin on her face.

"Whatever are you staring at, John?" she asked, bending forward.

"Looks like the moon's about ready to come out," Slocum said, going to her and tugging down the frilly bloomers to expose the half moons of her rump. He ran his hands over the sleek, taut skin and felt the way Abigail trembled now.

But when he undid his shirt and started unbuttoning his jeans, she moved away from him.

"What's wrong?" he asked.

"Nothing," Abigail said. "Get out of those clothes. And come outside."

"It's raining," he protested.

"We both need a bath. How better to take one than with each other?"

She wiggled free of her bloomers and stood completely naked beside the door. Abigail trembled a little as the rain came through the door and hit her bare flesh.

"It feels good. It's still warm. If it turns cold, we can come back inside."

"I want to be inside," Slocum said, shucking off his boots and getting out of his jeans.

"My, my, you're ready for anything, aren't you?" she said, staring at his groin. Then Abigail agilely twisted past the broken door and went outside into the rain. Slocum followed. She was right about the rain being warm, but the constant spattering against him distracted him from the ivory nymph running around outside the house, arms high over her head, laughing and twirling around and around so the rain found every part of her body.

Slocum made his way through the mud to her. Abigail's bare skin gleamed with clean water. He watched the rivulets form and run down her face, off her long blond hair, down between her huge breasts—and then sneak over her belly on their way still lower. Slocum stepped closer. This time Abigail didn't try to escape from him.

Their lips met and crushed together in a passionate kiss. Arms circling one another's body, they rubbed wetly against each other. Slocum felt the sleek, slick movement of her nipples across his bare chest and the way her inner thigh slid along his as she moved even closer. His manhood pressed hard against her crotch, but he did not enter her.

He was too tall for easy entry, but at the moment he hardly noticed. His hands ran over her wet body, seeking to stimulate every inch of flesh he could. When he came to her rounded behind, he cupped those fleshy mounds and then squeezed down hard.

Abigail let out a tiny sob of pleasure and seemed to melt. The rain fell harder on them, dousing them both. Slocum enjoyed the stimulation of the rain on his back and hair, but the feel of the woman's body thrilled him more. He grew as hard as steel and needed more of her than he was getting.

"Yes, John, I know. I'm ready. I'm as wet inside as I am out!"

He cupped her buttocks and lifted powerfully. Abigail threw her other leg around his waist and locked her heels

behind his back. Her arms circled his neck as she kissed
and licked and nipped at his lips and ears. Slocum was
more intent on positioning her hips than he was on relishing the feel of her taut nips against him or the way she
used her mouth so erotically.

He bounced her up and down a few times. Without
even realizing he had done so, he positioned her exactly.
As Abigail's body lowered, he felt the tangled matt of
fleecy blond fur between her legs tickle his shaft. Then
he plunged deep within her, surging far into her most
intimate nook. The shock of entry caused them both to
gasp and simply stand motionless, intense emotions robbing them of volition.

In the rain, water running down their naked bodies, they
stood for an eternity reveling in the sensations of heat and
moistness and sexual tension. The pressure around Slocum's fleshy pillar grew as Abigail clamped down with
her strong inner muscles. Then she began twisting from
side to side.

"Now, John. I'm ready. Do it now."

Slocum lifted her until only the thick purpled knob on
his shaft remained within her, then he relaxed and left
gravity pull her down. The slow withdrawal and the sudden insertion built carnal heat to the point where Slocum
thought he was going to explode.

He refused to give in so easily and wanted the most
pleasure possible from their lovemaking. He stroked over
her back, kissed her mouth and eyes and forehead and
then got a better grip on her buttocks. With the rain pum-
meling them both now, he bent his knees and straightened
them. The combination of the rain trickling sensuously
down their bodies, the feel of Slocum's massive shaft
within and the way he held her so close caused Abigail
to gasp in ecstasy.

"Oh, John, yes, I—aieee!" She threw her head back,
face to the plummeting warm rain, and let her hair dangle

down behind her. This slammed her groin down harder into his so he sank even deeper into her heated tunnel. The twitches and twists of her hips as she writhed about impaled on his fleshy spike ignited the potent forces of passion within her young body.

Abigail cried out in wild abandon, turned into a fierce, struggling animal that knew only physical delight. As her climax cascaded through her body, she clenched even harder around his hidden steely length. Slocum tried to pull out for one more fast, hard trip in but couldn't. He felt himself tightening, the floods beginning and then releasing as if a dam had burst. Swinging her around and around, he experienced the same joys she had moments earlier.

Slocum wasn't certain how long the delightful sensations racked his body, but he eventually released her and Abigail slid her feet to the ground. They stood ankle-deep in mud but neither noticed that or the heavy rain that now pounded them relentlessly. They kissed and caressed and explored each other's bare body until they were ready to go into the sod house and continue in a more traditional fashion.

The rain kept up its steady downpour all night. Slocum and Abigail matched it, their lightning and thunder more exciting.

10

"As nice as it is to find you out here, I've got to ask why you're traveling alone across the prairie," Slocum said, leaning back on his bedroll spread across the dirt floor of the sod house. Abigail busied herself stretching out her clothing to hang and dry from a bit of rope strung from one side of the room to the other. Every move she made distracted Slocum since she was buck naked, but he tried to keep his mind on why he was here.

Rafe Ferguson wasn't going to get by with trying to bushwhack him. And if Ferguson hadn't been the one pulling the trigger, he knew who had. The mayor and Ferguson were in cahoots, and in spite of the way he felt toward Abigail, Slocum had to wonder if she was in the plot with them.

"There're so many of the farmers to convince, John," Abigail said, half turning so she was limned by the faint morning light coming through the door. This gave him a delightful view of her bare breasts and the flare of her rump in silhouette. "The directors won't need a complete agreement but most of the countryside has to agree or there will be trouble."

"There's already trouble brewing," Slocum said. He

91

turned from her so her nakedness wouldn't distract him.

"What do you mean?" Abigail came and sat beside him on the floor, her warm leg pressing into his side. There wasn't any way he could keep from being distracted now.

"The mayor is cooking up a scheme with Rafe Ferguson. Ferguson is a swindler. The two of them together spell big trouble for No Consequence and the train." He went on to tell her how no one in Omaha had heard of a railroad spur being run in this direction.

"I can't answer that, John," she said, looking thoughtful. Then her face brightened. "It might be that Mr. Westfall is keeping it under his hat so other towns won't compete with us. There are any number that'd steal away such an opportunity. The county seat—Seneca," she hurried on, warming to her theory. "They would be a ghost town in a year after we get the railroad here. They might think they deserve it because that's where the sheriff lives."

"Westfall said something similar, but I don't buy it," Slocum said. There wouldn't have been any reason for the back-shooter to make the attempt on his life if any part of the railroad yarn was true. Westfall and Ferguson wanted to shut him up permanently before he spooked the farmers—and Abigail.

"You can be so ornery, John," she said with mock severity. "You've got to think big. See how this is going to help us all."

Slocum had heard religious folk and knew arguing with them got nowhere. Abigail had the same conviction. No argument he might give would carry any weight in her need to believe that the railroad was coming through No Consequence.

"I've lost any chance at tracking the owlhoot who tried to kill me," Slocum said. "Reckon I can ride along with you until you get back to town."

Abigail was quiet for a moment, then bit her lower lip

before saying, "John? Will you promise me you won't try to argue against the railroad? I don't want you riding with me if I have to debate the point in front of every farmer and rancher I see."

"I could be wrong," Slocum admitted, but he had a feeling deep in his gut that he wasn't.

"Good," she said, all smiles now. "Let's get back in the saddle again."

"All right," Slocum said, reaching for her. "Then we can get dressed and ride on." He pulled the willing blonde down and showed her what it felt like to ride a bucking bronco.

"I'm so pleased at your confidence in the project, Mr. Kingman," Abigail said, positively glowing as she clutched the farmer's small bag of silver. "You're guaranteeing the future of not only the town but your own children."

Behind the sodbuster stood four young boys and two girls almost as tall as their mother. Slocum wondered what the farmer's wife thought of handing over their life savings to buy a railroad bond. He also wondered what Kingman and his family would do if the bond proved worthless. Life in Nebraska was hardscrabble at the best of times, the short-grass prairie chary in yielding wheat and corn.

"You sure them director fellas are comin' to town this weekend?" Kingman asked. "I don't feel good 'bout any deal less I kin look 'em in the eye."

"The mayor will introduce them, and they'll make the announcement that the Platte and Central Plains Railroad is coming to No Consequence." Abigail beamed. "We're going to need another vote, one to change the name."

"How's that, Miss Stanley?" asked the farmer's wife.

"No Consequence should be changed to Consequence!"

This produced relieved smiles from the adults. Slocum

saw the children weren't caught up in the discussion of the prosperity to be brought to the small town. They were more interested in getting to their chores so they could run off and throw stones into the stock tank or do whatever they wanted when they weren't working.

"This Saturday. Noon," Abigail promised. "Be prepared for one of Mr. Westfall's long-winded speeches. But this time, it'll be worth it!"

Abigail and Slocum mounted and rode back in the direction of town. They had visited five farms and Abigail had sweet-talked every last one of the men into buying the railroad bonds. Almost five hundred dollars in silver and scrip rode in her saddlebags, making Slocum glad he had chosen to stick with her. He still had a score to settle, but protecting Abigail and her money was more important.

He had a feeling Ferguson wasn't going to stray too far.

"How much have you raised for the railroad bonds?" Slocum asked. "All told?"

"Well, I suppose it is all right for me to tell you. We have more than met our subscription total. The extra money will go into an emergency fund, should it be required. Unexpected expenses always crop up."

"You know about these things?" Slocum asked. "You ever been around a railroad construction crew?"

"Oh, you're worried about what the roughnecks might do in town." Abigail breathed a sigh of relief. "We're expecting this. Mr. Westfall has it well in hand, he says. The saloons might do a land office business, but that's good for the town. My store is chocked full of supplies the crews will need for the first month or so. Profits ought to soar after a week, when I've gotten my expenses back."

"You've got it all worked out," Slocum said.

"This is a major project, John," she said earnestly. The blonde pushed back bangs creeping across her forehead

and into her eyes. He saw how she was looking at the
horizon, but she didn't see the storm clouds billowing
there. All Abigail saw was promise, opportunity, success.

"Did you come up with it or was this the mayor's brain-
child?"

"You do go on, don't you, John? I can't really say
whose idea it was. Several of us had been discussing the
matter for some time. I'm sure Mr. Westfall had a hand
in those discussions, but I don't remember him being the
one to suggest it originally." She frowned and then said,
"I'm sure Adam wasn't the one who thought bringing the
railroad to town would be a good idea. It was one of the
saloon owners. Maybe it was Paul Gorman."

"I can see how they would benefit," Slocum said, lost
in thought as they rode toward town. He knew he might
be wrong about the enterprise, but he doubted it.

"This works out so well. No Consequence sells the rev-
enue bonds, which are backed by the town's assets and
the income of its citizens. Taxes on everything shipped in
help pay for the interest and go to retire the principal.
And everyone benefits who ships out grain, cattle or other
goods because transportation is cheap and we can finally
compete with towns like North Platte."

"You've got it all wrapped up in a pretty bow," he said.

"You aren't convinced." Abigail heaved a deep sigh.
From the corner of his eye Slocum watched her breasts
rise and fall in exasperation. "Very well. I wasn't supposed to let anyone know until this weekend but the directors are already in town."

"What?" This brought Slocum around in the saddle.
"Where? In the hotel?"

"Hardly. People would flock to see them. No, they're
camped outside town a few miles."

"I didn't see them on the Omaha road when I came in,"
he said.

"Oh, they didn't come directly from there. That would

be too obvious. People would wonder why directors of the Platte and Central Plains Railroad were heading toward a town without a spur line. No, they went to North Platte and rode up from there."

"Clever," Slocum said, remembering how no one in Omaha admitted to there even being a Platte & Central Plains Railroad.

"You still sound skeptical. We'll meet them, before they are inundated with questions from everyone else in town. Oh, John, this is so exciting. I feel like I have just discovered a new mountain no one else has ever seen before or an ocean, perhaps. This must be the way Frémont felt on his expeditions!"

Slocum rode in silence as Abigail waxed eloquent about the benefits to the entire region and how they would try to be charitable toward the neighboring town of Seneca, even graciously allowing Seneca to remain the county seat in spite of No Consequence being the important rail center.

"There," Abigail cried, standing in the stirrups and pointing into the distance. Haze obscured the flat grasslands, but Slocum thought he made out a thin curl of smoke rising from a camp fire. "They're camped right where they said they would."

Abigail sounded almost hopeful that this would convince Slocum he was wrong about everything. He had started to answer when he saw dust rising off to his left. Squinting, Slocum shielded his eyes from the hot Nebraska sun and tried to make out who rode about a mile off. A solitary rider.

The back-shooter who had missed him in No Consequence? Slocum couldn't tell. He considered riding out to see if this might be Rafe Ferguson, then Abigail decided the matter for him.

"Hallo!" the woman cried, waving her arms about like a berserk windmill. "There, John, see? It's them. The directors, just where they said they'd be. Come on!"

Abigail put her spurs to her horse and shot off like a rocket. Slocum followed at a more leisurely pace, eyes hunting for the rider off in the distance. His roan neighed as they neared the camp with the fire fed by burning buffalo chips, but Slocum held it steady. The rider he had spotted earlier had vanished.

"Here he is," Abigail gushed. She had already dismounted and stood in front of a well-dressed man who stood with his back to Slocum. She clung to the man's hand, pumping it up and down like a thirsty woman expecting to get water from a well. "That's my good friend, John Slocum. John, I want you to meet the chairman of the board of the Platte and Central Plains Railroad, Mr. Lawrence Beal."

The man turned slowly, Abigail following him around, never letting go of his hand, as if this were a lifeline and if she let go she would drown.

Somehow, Slocum wasn't surprised to be facing one of the men he had seen Rafe Ferguson gambling with in the saloon back in North Platte.

11

"Where's your friend?" Slocum asked, not bothering to take Beal's hand as the man reached out to shake.

"My friend? What friend is that? Have we met?" Beal looked at Abigail as if she had led him into a trap. From the flash of fear that changed to irritation, he knew Beal wasn't on the level. Convincing Abigail was something Slocum couldn't figure out how to do.

"Maybe I was mistaken," Slocum said. "I thought I saw you talking to Rafe Ferguson in a saloon back in North Platte. A week or two back. There was another man with you in a poker game." Slocum stepped to one side and caught a glimpse of another man all gussied up in finery sitting inside the tent, hunched over a table and talking earnestly with a hayseed farmer.

"Oh, perhaps you mean Mr. Quenton. He is my associate on the board of directors."

"Of the Platte and Central Plains Railroad," Slocum finished, a note of sarcasm in his voice. Beal chose to ignore it and rattled on.

"It is with some pleasure we have come to your fine part of the country. No Consequence will make a fine terminus for a spur line."

"All the way from your rail yards in Omaha?" asked Slocum. This time Beal tensed and moved his hand to the left lapel of his coat, as if he was going to strike an orator's pose. Slocum saw the tiny bulge in the man's coat and knew Beal was going for a derringer, if Slocum pressed him too much.

"That's right. From our yards in Omaha. Your attitude is peculiar, sir," Beal said coldly. He turned to Abigail and said, "I trust your mission has proven successful. With acquaintances such as him, it must have been a doubly difficult chore."

"Oh, Mr. Beal, don't pay any attention to John. He doesn't have the vision others have."

"You both have the vision, Miss Stanley, and are a vision. Of loveliness, that is." Beal smiled ingratiatingly, and Slocum wanted to punch him out. Abigail ate up the compliments.

"I've got the money from bond sales here."

"No, no," Beal said. "Mr. Quenton and I don't get the money. Legally, this is money raised by your community and backed by the full faith of No Consequence's taxing power. Mr. Westfall is the gentleman who handles such money."

"Until it's time to build the railroad?" asked Slocum. "Does the money go into escrow until it is used?"

"What are you saying, John? That something's not right? Why, you can be so suspicious at times. No," Abigail said hurriedly, "the money is in the bank and will be doled out at every stage of the construction."

"That's right. The initial construction from Omaha onto the prairie will be done using Platte and Central Plains funds," Beal said. "Only when we get within ten miles of No Consequence will we be eligible for the funds raised by the municipal bonds."

"See, John? You thought Mr. Beal was some sort of a

crook. He—his company—won't see a penny of the bond money until they are almost here."

"That guarantees each party of the probity of the other," Beal said. "We are risking a considerable amount of time and capital building near No Consequence, but the railroad would be of no use to the town unless tracks come to the depot. And the Platte and Central Plains Railroad gets no money unless we finish that final few miles."

"That seems fair," Slocum said, wondering if he was barking up the wrong tree. "What'd you have to say to Ferguson back in North Platte?"

"Why, if I remember rightly, he wanted a job with our company. I'm not in personnel. That's more in Mr. Quenton's department." Beal half turned. Slocum stiffened, thinking Beal was going for the derringer in his vest pocket, but when the man turned back, his hand still rested on his broad coat lapel.

"What's the ruckus?" Quenton came from the tent, his arm around the farmer's shoulders. The farmer looked a little dazed but had a grin on his face as if he had been on a three-day drunk. "I just completed negotiations with Mr. Garrett here for use of his farmland."

"They's gonna pay me five thousand dollars," the man said, his eyes wide in wonder. His smile got even goofier. "Imagine that. I ain't growed half that in crops since I been in Nebraska."

"You'll have to buy us all a drink back in town," Slocum said.

"Wall, I ain't got the money yet. That comes out of the bond money Miss Stanley and the rest're raisin'." Before Slocum could say anything, the farmer went on. "I reckon the bonds're durn good investments. And dangnabit, I'm gonna be rich, so I bought a hunnred dollars' worth myself."

The bulge in Quenton's pocket told how Garrett had paid—in cash.

"You won't regret it, Mr. Garrett," Abigail said, her smile matching the farmer's. "Your return on the investment will be substantial."

"We have a great deal of work to do, Miss Stanley," Beal said, inclining his head slightly in the direction of the tent. "If you and Mr. Slocum will excuse us . . ."

"Of course. I only wanted for John to meet you."

"What about the money you took from Garrett?" Slocum asked. "You gents don't have anything to do with the bonds, do you?"

"Why, no, as I explained to you earlier we don't," Beal said with ill grace. "Let Miss Stanley take the money you collected into town."

Quenton's hand went to the bulge in his pocket. For an instant he froze, as if undecided. Then he pulled out the wad of greenbacks and passed it over to Abigail, who took it and placed it with the rest of the money in her saddlebags.

"I'll see that you get the actual bond certificate, Mr. Garrett. Ride into town with us and I'll ask Mr. Carleton to issue it immediately, even before the others." She patted the saddlebags to show how many others were ahead of Garrett but that he was a special case. This pleased the farmer and made Slocum shake his head.

Everything sounded aboveboard, but with Rafe Ferguson mixed up in it, how could this deal be legitimate? Worse, Slocum had learned to obey his gut instincts. That had kept him alive since the war, and right now his belly churned every time he looked at Quenton or Beal.

"Who can authorize the release of the money to Beal and Quenton?" Slocum asked as they found the road into No Consequence. Garrett rode his mule some distance behind, so Slocum felt he could talk in private with Abigail without getting her unduly upset over his attitude.

"You never let up, do you, John? It's all legal. I made sure by asking a lawyer down in North Platte about it. No

Consequence has the authority to issue the bonds, and I'm not so stupid as to allow anyone to get the money until the railroad comes in."

"Can the mayor dole it out?"

"Of course not. He has to have permission of the town council. Then, when they are in agreement that the Platte and Central Plains has lived up to their end of the deal, Mr. Carleton is told to release the money. Even then, it is only a portion for every mile laid, with the bulk being paid out when an engine steams into the No Consequence depot."

"Sounds like you've covered every possibility," Slocum said. He rode in silence, wondering why the churning in his belly wouldn't go away. If the railroad wasn't built, no money would be released.

Still . . .

"Here's the bank, Mr. Garrett," Abigail called to the mule-riding farmer. "We're just in time. It won't close for another few minutes." She turned to Slocum and gave him a faint smile. "I wish I could convince you this is for the good of everyone in town, John."

He didn't answer. She slipped from the saddle, took the money she had collected and made certain she had her neatly written list of those buying the municipal bonds, then went inside with the farmer.

Slocum wasted no time turning his roan's face and heading back along the road they had just ridden. He made the best speed he could returning to the directors' camp. Without Abigail and Garrett to get in the way, Slocum reckoned he could get some straight answers from the two railroad company directors. But he drew rein and sat stock-still, intently watching as a lone rider crossed the short-grass prairie and made a beeline for the tents.

Even at this distance Slocum recognized Adam Westfall.

Figuring the meeting might be more interesting if they

didn't know he was listening, Slocum jumped from the saddle and tethered his horse to a clump of yucca, then advanced on foot to find a decent spot to eavesdrop. A deep wash ran close to the campsite, giving him the chance to get within ten yards without being seen. The rest of the way, Slocum had to use his skills to creep forward.

Beal, Quenton and Westfall were in the largest of the tents, sitting at the table where Quenton had convinced the farmer they were going to give him a king's ransom in exchange for his land.

"Don't hog that bottle," complained Westfall. "It's a long, dusty ride from town and I need to wet my whistle."

"You haven't been working like we have," answered Quenton. "I should have gotten drunk before I started talking to all those farmers. Damn, but they stink worse than I remember.".

"How'd you know, with that smelly perfume you use?" Beal asked.

"It's not perfume," Quenton said testily. "It's called *eau de toilette* and came all the way from Paris, France."

"I don't care what fancy-ass name you call it, it still smells like something died," shot back Beal.

"Quit your bellyaching," said Adam Westfall. "Let's get down to it."

Glasses clinked and three gurgling sounds reached Slocum. He flopped onto his belly and peered under the edge of the canvas. The trio sat at the table, a bottle of brandy between them. They raised their glasses in a toast.

"To being filthy rich!" Quenton cried.

"To money," chimed in Westfall. Beal said nothing, too intent on knocking back his drink so he could pour himself another.

For a few minutes they were too eager to see how much of the liquor they could consume to say much, but Westfall finally belched and leaned back in his chair, hooked his thumb in his belt and stared at the other two men.

"When's he going to get here? I don't have all day."

"He's on his way," said Beal. "What do you have to do other than covet all that money sitting in the bank?"

"I hear a horse coming. That might be him." Quenton shot to his feet and went to the tent flap and pushed it back. Slocum was at the rear of the tent but worried the newcomer might spot him. He lay still and tense, ready to go for his six-shooter if any of the men noticed him. They were too intent on other matters to notice, including the man who joined them inside. Slocum's eyes went wide in surprise when he saw the banker strut into the tent.

He had expected to see Rafe Ferguson.

"Howdy, gents," Carleton said. "I waited a spell to close up the bank." He laughed. "I had to take more money off that stupid bitch and her dumb friend, so it was worth my while."

"*Our* while." Quenton sounded a tad touchy about it, making Slocum wonder if there was already a falling out among the thieves.

"All our whiles," Westfall said. "Sit down and have a drink. We've got another hour to kill before he gets here."

"Why do we need him?" complained Carleton.

"Ferguson put it all together," Beal said. "And we don't cross him. Quenton and I've seen what happens if anybody tries. There was a deal that went sour back in Kansas City . . ."

Slocum didn't stick around to hear any more. He had been right all along. Rafe Ferguson was in cahoots with the mayor and town banker, as well as the two bogus railroad directors, and intended to steal the money Abigail had raised. The only way Slocum could see to convince her of the plot was to let her listen herself. Since No Consequence didn't have a marshal, getting the law involved wasn't going to be easy.

He figured that when Abigail got her dander up, the

law would pale in comparison. She was likely to rally the townspeople and farmers and lynch the lot of the conspirators. But first she had to be convinced.

Slocum reached his stallion, vaulted into the saddle and galloped for No Consequence. Once or twice along the way, he debated the wisdom of taking Abigail back to spy on Westfall and the others, then finally convinced himself it was the only proof she would accept. The men had to condemn themselves.

He hit the ground running in front of Abigail's store. She was working at the back of the store, the rear door open so he could see that she was moving supplies from a large shed. She looked up when he came in and smiled. A quick swipe of her handkerchief mopped up some of the sweat on her forehead.

"I'm glad you're here, John. Can you help me move the sacks of flour? I've had them out back and I'm afraid weevils are getting into—" She saw his expression. "What's wrong?"

"You have to see this and hear it yourself," Slocum said. "Otherwise, you'd never believe me."

"That's not true. You—" Abigail bit off her denial and stared wide-eyed at him. She ran both hands through her mussed-up blond hair and glared. "This has to do with the railroad, doesn't it?"

"You listen and you decide."

"I don't know. Will it take long? I have so much work to do before the railroad crews start asking for supplies."

"Not long," he said. "Your horse is still saddled and we only have to go back to the directors' camp."

"Very well," she said, wiping her hands on an apron, "but this had better not be a wild goose chase, John."

"If it is, I won't say another word about the railroad spur," Slocum promised.

"It's worth taking a few minutes off, just for that," she said, smiling a little now. She grabbed her hat and went out back to get her horse. Slocum waited impatiently for her out front of the store.

"Ride hard. We probably have plenty of time, but I want to be sure," he said. Slocum checked his watch and saw it had taken him only twenty minutes to get into No Consequence. With his roan tiring, it might take longer to return. He wanted to be in position to overhear everything when Rafe Ferguson showed up.

Abigail would have irrefutable proof that this was a hoax that would cost the people of No Consequence a hundred thousand dollars.

"Do we have to rush so, John? I'm tuckered out from being on the trail for so long." She bent forward and kept pace with Slocum in spite of her complaint.

"Ferguson is joining them. I want you to hear what they all say."

"Ferguson? I don't understand."

Slocum maintained the pace and didn't bother answering. Conversation was hard and he didn't want to say the wrong thing and cause Abigail to return to town without hearing the scoundrels implicate themselves in the plot.

"Here," he said, finding the spot where he had left his horse before. "You'll have some rough going when we come up on the tent, but don't make a sound. Just listen."

"What am I supposed to hear, John? Tell me."

"I don't want to sway you. Just stay out of sight and reach your own conclusions."

He took her hand as they made their way along the deep wash. Slocum had to help Abigail up the crumbling embankment, and she almost cried out when he pushed her flat into the dirt. Grass crushed under her and stained her clothing. But she fell silent without any urging when she peeped under the tent and saw Carleton, Westfall and the two railroad men drunk at the table.

"She's a bitch, you know," Carleton said drunkenly,

"but 'bout the purtiest blond filly I ever did see. Wonder what she'd be like between the sheets."

"The very idea," Abigail hissed. "How dare they talk about anyone like that!"

Slocum put his hand on her arm to keep her quiet. Then he had to hold her back.

"Abigail's a purty name," Carleton said. "For a whore. Wonder if she'd leave that store of hers if I offered her five dollars for a tumble in the hay?"

"You could offer her a hundred and she'd never bed you," Westfall said. "Now me, I've had her a half dozen times. She's not that good, not like the really expensive fancy women in St. Louis."

"Why that—" Abigail seethed and forced Slocum to clamp his hand over her mouth. She jerked away angrily and hissed, "He's lying! He and I never—"

Slocum put his finger to his lips to silence her, then jabbed his finger in the direction of the tent flap. Abigail had been so angry she hadn't heard Rafe Ferguson ride up.

"Howdy, gents," Ferguson said, swinging into the tent and sitting down so his back was to the tent entrance. He almost faced Slocum and Abigail where they peered up from under the canvas at the rear of the tent.

" 'Bout time you showed," Quenton said, drunkenly slurring his words. "We need to decide when the time's right for takin' the money and gettin' the hell out of this jerkwater town."

"Jerkwater," laughed Ferguson. "That's rich. There'll never be a railroad in No Consequence. Hell, they don't even have water enough for a stock tank, much less a steam engine."

"The only thing I want to be rich is me," Carleton said. "If we wait till Westfall finishes speaking at the rally, we might die of old age."

"You are a windbag, Westfall," Beal confirmed needlessly. He almost toppled from his chair. The brandy bottle was empty, and Beal looked as if he had consumed most of its contents.

Slocum waited to hear the details and was taken by surprise when Abigail jerked away, lifted the back of the tent and scrambled inside.

"You all should be ashamed of yourselves!" she cried.

Slocum knew the fat was in the fire now when the men went for their hideout guns.

12

A thousand thoughts flashed through Slocum's mind, and nothing but death seemed a likely outcome. He hated running in the face of trouble, but getting himself ventilated wouldn't help Abigail. Slocum pushed back and let the edge of the tent drop, leaving the blonde inside with the angry, armed outlaws.

He scrambled backward on his belly, rolled onto his side and then got to his feet. The Colt Navy came easily to hand, but he faced too many armed men—and from the sounds inside the tent, they had taken Abigail prisoner. Any shootout he started now would quickly end the impetuous woman's life.

"How dare you?" he heard Abigail cry from inside the tent. Her outraged question was followed quickly by a loud slap.

Slocum didn't know who had hit Abigail, and it didn't much matter to him. They would all pay.

"She didn't come here alone. Where's Slocum?" demanded Adam Westfall.

"Slocum? Slocum's after us?" This came from Rafe Ferguson. "Son of a bitch, why didn't you say something about that? I thought he was dead. You said you'd take care of him, Westfall."

"Your man missed," the mayor said. "I was damned surprised when I saw he was still alive and kicking."

"Why didn't you tell me?"

"There wasn't time. We—"

"Shut up," snapped Beal. "We got the woman. And Slocum's around somewhere. Let's get him!"

"Why bother?" asked Quenton. The way he spoke sent a shiver down Slocum's spine. The others were hot under the collar and likely to make mistakes, but Quenton thought things out. Slocum knew what the man was going to say, and it didn't set well with him. Not at all.

Slocum jumped into the ravine and raced back to where he and Abigail had left their horses. He couldn't shoot it out with Ferguson and the others without the woman being killed. Surrendering was out of the question, and this was exactly what Quenton would demand: surrender or they would shoot Abigail.

If Slocum gave himself up, they would kill both of them and bury their bodies out on the prairie.

Out of breath but determined, Slocum swung into the saddle and bent low to grab the reins to Abigail's horse. He jerked hard to get the mare away from a tasty clump of blue grama, then put his heels to his roan's flanks and got it walking back up the ravine toward the tents.

As he rode, he fumbled in his pocket for the tin of lucifers he carried. It had been a spell since he'd bought any tobacco for a smoke, and he had given what he had to the Sioux, but the smoke he intended now was going to be a damned sight bigger than a cigarette. Working feverishly, he finally got the match lit. He held it, worrying that he was doing something foolish. The he worried it wouldn't be enough.

"Slocum!" called Ferguson. "We got your lady here. Now, we don't want to hurt her. You know that. But

Westfall and Carleton have a letch for her. That'd be mighty unpleasant for the lady."

The mayor and banker protested, but Slocum didn't have to see what was going on to know Beal and Quenton had silenced them while their boss dictated his demands.

"You give yourself up and we let the little lady go. Unharmed. Unmolested by these two fine, upstanding citizens. And from the way they're looking at her, they're really upstanding right about now. What do you say, Slocum? Give up!"

Slocum watched the lucifer sputter and sizzle. He tossed it to the ground, where it immediately found a clump of dried grass. Almost as if he'd had another wish granted, a sudden puff of wind fanned the flame into a raging fire that spread directly for the camp.

"Fire!" shouted Carleton. The banker and mayor knew the danger of a prairie fire and bolted for their horses. The momentary confusion afforded Slocum all the opening he needed.

Head down, he spurred his horse through the sheet of flame already licking at the rear of the tent.

"Abigail!" he shouted.

Ferguson was taken by surprise and let Abigail jerk free. But he recovered fast and went for his six-gun. Slocum didn't give him time. A heavy boot lashed out and caught Ferguson under the chin, sending him reeling backward into Beal and Quenton. The trio went down in a heap.

"John, let's go." Abigail was flushed and breathless from her brief captivity. She quickly mounted one of the horses. "I want to get to Seneca and herd that worthless sheriff out here to arrest those crooks!"

Slocum saw they had doubled their trouble in only a few seconds. The heat from behind was too intense to permit escape the way he had come. Ferguson and Quenton were dragging out their guns, Ferguson a six-gun and Quenton a small pepperbox. Adding to the confusion, the wind tore the tent loose from its stakes and blew it across the area right in front of the men.

"That way," Slocum said, pointing in the direction already taken by Westfall and Carleton.

"I want them. Oh, how I want to tear them apart with my bare hands! I'll claw out their lying eyes! I'll—"

Slocum didn't care what motivated Abigail as long as she rode hard and fast. He followed her through the confusion. Whether it was a slug from one of the men's guns or a piece of wood exploding in the heat from the fire, Slocum neither knew nor cared as it blasted past his head. Keeping low, he fought his way into the wall of flame.

"Keep riding. Not that way, to your right, do it, Abigail, now!" he shouted at the woman. She was too intent on trailing the mayor and banker to notice she would be cut off by the fire.

"I want them, John. I won't let them go!"

This time Slocum was sure it was hot lead that sang past him. He touched his arm, and his fingers came away damp with his own blood. Ferguson wasn't a good shot, but with the amount of lead he was flinging in Slocum's direction, he didn't have to be. A shriller, more insistent shot rang out, quickly followed by Quenton's curses. The pepperbox had discharged all four rounds as it blew up in his hand.

Slocum's horse took a low ravine with ease and then they were in fresher air. He chanced a look over his shoulder to see the flames devour the tent. The thick, oily grass smoke cloaked the camp, but Slocum thought he saw two riders making their way to safety.

"How dare they say such lies about me?" raged Abigail. "And they're cooking up some scheme to steal the bond money!"

"Whoa," Slocum said, reining back. His roan was tiring fast from too much galloping. The prairie fire still raged, but it began to turn, following the wash. If Slocum remembered the lay of the land, it would reach a rocky stretch and burn itself out. He was glad he hadn't set a fire that would burn hundreds of thousands of acres.

More than this, he was glad he and Abigail were still alive and in one piece.

"Are you convinced they're out to dupe the people of No Consequence?" he asked.

"You were right, John. I should have trusted your instincts, but I wanted it so badly. I saw all the communiqués. I don't know how I could have been fooled like that. It all looked so real!"

"Ferguson is expert at swindling," Slocum said. He wiped his face and came away with equal amounts of sweat, soot and blood. A flying hunk of wood had scratched his forehead and he had never noticed until now.

"I'll get them. Oh!" Abigail was beside herself with anger.

Slocum turned his horse in a full circle. The fire had died to a smelly, smoky charring of dead grass; he worried more about the two directors and Rafe Ferguson. They could take care of the mayor and Carleton later, but the three men posed the real danger, if they caught up with Slocum out on the prairie. With or without a pepperbox, the trio could still outgun him.

"Are you mad at them for what they said about you or do you want to stop their scheme?"

"I—What's the difference?" Abigail's jaw firmed and from the flinty look in her blue eyes, Slocum knew Westfall and Carleton were in for a whale of a hard time. Being sent to prison would be the least of their punishment.

"None, I reckon. We'll have to swing wide to get back to town," Slocum said, "but it's better if we go straight for Seneca."

"Why?" Abigail was already heading back toward No Consequence.

"The county sheriff. You need to get a lawman."

"There'll be time for that. If I have to get together a vigilante committee, I'll do it. But I won't give them time to hightail it out of town. That fool of a sheriff could never track them down—he wouldn't even try."

"Maybe not, but he'll stand a better chance of catching them red-handed if we get him now." Slocum heaved a sigh and turned from the road toward Seneca when it became apparent Abigail was going back to No Consequence, come hell or high water.

He trotted alongside, letting the woman seethe in silence. Slocum considered what was likely to happen when they reached town and knew there would probably be bloodshed. He touched the butt of his six-shooter and hoped the mayor and banker had kept running.

"Look at that, John. I don't believe it!"

Slocum frowned when he saw the mayor on a podium in front of city hall haranguing a small crowd of townspeople. The words sparked some interest in the gathering, but Slocum couldn't hear what was being said. He didn't think he would like it.

"Stay here," he told Abigail. "I'll see to Westfall."

"No." The woman was adamant about facing down the mayor and reached the back of the crowd before he did.

"Adam Westfall, you're a scoundrel!" Abigail cried. "You're out to steal all these good people's money, you and Carleton! And those phony railroad directors! And Rafe Ferguson! You're all in cahoots!"

"Miss Stanley, you are distraught. A touch of heat stroke?" Westfall suggested, looking unflustered by her accusations. Slocum knew sentiment wasn't on his and Abigail's side from the looks on the faces of the men and women in the crowd.

"He's trying to steal the money. I heard him scheming!" Abigail started to get tongue-tied as her rage mounted. She remembered what Westfall had claimed about her and him. Slocum wondered if there might not be a touch of truth somewhere in the mayor's bragging to his cronies, no matter what Abigail claimed.

"Miss Stanley, please. This is no place to make unwarranted claims. I was just informing these fine citizens of a new telegram from the directors, who will be arriving this weekend."

"They're your friends!" Abigail shouted, turning red in the face.

"Why, yes, I count them as my friends. We are certainly engaged in a business deal, but they are fine gentlemen." Westfall looked so smug Slocum wanted to punch him out.

"Rafe Ferguson is a swindler with a half dozen wanted posters chasing him," Slocum said. "You're working for him."

"Ferguson? I don't know anyone by that name," Westfall said coldly. "Do you share Miss Stanley's delusions, too, Slocum?"

"No delusion. The only mirage here is the railroad. It's not coming to No Consequence. Westfall intends to steal the money."

"We've been over this," Westfall said, holding out his hands to quiet the crowd. "Slocum thinks there is something amiss. There's not. Everything is set up to protect both No Consequence and the Platte and Central Plains Railroad."

"He's right," piped up Carleton. The portly bank president waddled up and shoved aside the mayor at the podium. "I don't like my honesty being challenged this way. Even if Mayor Westfall cut corners dealing with the railroad, I assure you all I will not release the money until the spur line is within ten miles of our depot. The railroad won't risk losing the money over a mere ten miles of track. We will get our railroad, ladies and gentleman! The mayor says so, and so do I!"

A cheer went up.

Slocum hesitated. He had hoped the mayor would keep riding once he had been flushed out on the prairie, but that hadn't happened. With the banker backing Westfall up, who in No Consequence would believe either him or Abigail? From the look of the crowd, the answer was apparent.

"Abigail," he said softly. "We're not getting anywhere." She didn't see the truth in his words.

"You're a crook, Adam Westfall! So are you, Edward Carleton!" She turned slightly in the saddle to address the crowd. "I was duped by them into raising the money. They're going to steal it. There aren't any railroad directors. Rafe Ferguson is behind it all. As Mr. Slocum said, Ferguson is a swindler second to none, and he is the puppeteer pulling these . . . these . . . terrible men's strings!"

"You're hysterical, Abigail," Westfall said. "Don't make a public scene. I don't know what happened but—"

"I'll stop you, Adam! You can't say such horrible untruths about me and steal the money and—"

Abigail lunged for the mayor, but Slocum grabbed her arm and kept her in the saddle. Their horses began pawing the ground skittishly as the crowd murmured its displeasure with them.

"Nobody's buying it," Slocum told her.

"I can't let them steal everyone's money!"

"You can't stop them on their own turf," Slocum pointed out.

Abigail jerked her arm free and spun around to face Westfall and Carleton. "You two will go to jail. I'll fetch the sheriff, and he'll arrest you!"

The crowd started turning ugly now. They no more wanted to have their hopes and dreams dashed than Abigail had before eavesdropping on the swindlers.

"Please, stay calm," Carleton urged. "There are always those who want to stop progress. But a woman with heat prostration and a cowboy? Will you listen to them or to your elected mayor?"

"And the president of your town bank," Westfall chimed in. "You can trust Ed Carleton. Mr. Carleton has been in No Consequence since the first building went up. We have our reputations on the line."

"The only line you'll ever see is a noose around your scrawny necks!" cried Abigail. "The sheriff will put an end to your thievery!"

Slocum saw that the threat carried some weight with the two men, in spite of the way they covered their discomfort with mention of the law coming to examine their railroad deal.

"Abigail, let's get out of town. Now."

Slocum doubted Abigail's neighbors would lynch her, but it wouldn't take much for Westfall to whip the crowd into a frenzy of anger against him since he was an interloper. Slocum reckoned he had a few more years of riding the trail before he cashed in. Kicking at the end of a lynch mob's rope wasn't the way he intended to go.

Abigail hissed like a mad cat and galloped away from the crowd, leaving behind a cloud of dust and ill feelings. Slocum followed at a slower pace but knew he wasn't likely to be welcome in No Consequence anytime soon.

Just outside town, Slocum caught up with the furious woman and grabbed her reins to bring her to a halt so they could talk.

"You'd better do some serious thinking what it means to get the sheriff," he told her. "You'll need more proof than the two of us overhearing what Beal, Quenton and those two owlhoots said." He jerked his thumb back in the direction of town.

"But we heard it, John."

"It's our word against theirs. A distraught woman and a drifter. A popular elected mayor and a banker who helped found the town. Who's the sheriff going to listen to?"

"But they—they!" Abigail began sputtering as her rage grew.

"All I'm saying is that you'd better have solid proof. Nobody in Omaha has ever heard of the Platte and Central Plains Railroad. That's a start. Beal and Quenton are frauds. That can be determined by the sheriff sending a telegram to Omaha. What else is there? You were the one who raised the most money for this bogus railroad. You ought to know."

"Oh, John. What if they accuse me?" Abigail put her hand to her throat.

"That's not too likely, but something to think on," Slocum said.

"It'll take us a day or so to reach Seneca. We can work out what we're going to say by then. But we'd better start soon. I don't want them hightailing it before the sheriff can get here."

"They can't run too far in a couple days," Slocum said. He knew frightened men like Westfall and Carleton would leave a trail a blind man could follow. Rafe Ferguson was another matter. He was an old hand at such swindles and knew all the ways of vanishing without a trace to keep the law off him.

Slocum decided he would let the sheriff follow the mayor and banker. He would take care of Ferguson personally.

He had swung his horse around to head for the county seat at Seneca when he heard the distinctive sound of a rifle cocking.

He didn't have to find Rafe Ferguson. Ferguson had found him.

13

"I ought to shoot you down right here and now, Slocum. The last time our paths crossed you almost got my head stuck into a noose. How's it feel to have the tables turned?" Rafe Ferguson kept the rifle aimed squarely at Slocum's chest, ready to fire if Slocum so much as twitched.

"You can't do this!" exclaimed Abigail.

"Don't count on it," Ferguson said, sneering. "Look behind you 'fore you get it into your pretty head to do anything dumb."

Slocum turned his head enough to see Beal and Quenton, both with rifles trained on Abigail and him. He had ridden into the trap with his eyes open because he had underestimated Ferguson and had thought the man would be halfway to the Rockies by now. The lure of the money tucked away in the bank was too big for a crook like Ferguson to pass up.

"We got you, Slocum. We really got you," Ferguson gloated. "Now you just turn that pony of yours and ride real slow back toward town. Keep your hands high, in case you think you can escape."

"Just shoot us and get it over," Slocum said. "Or should

I turn my back to give you your usual target?"

"I didn't take that shot at you, but if I had, I wouldn't have missed," Ferguson said, his face turning livid with anger. His finger twitched on the rifle trigger. Slocum tensed, ready for whatever opening Ferguson might afford him. If the swindler fired, both Slocum's and Abigail's horses would rear and make them more difficult targets.

Slocum might also end up with a slug in him, but he saw no other way out of the trap.

Ferguson laughed harshly.

"There'll be plenty of time for you to die, Slocum. Ride ahead of us real slow-like."

Slocum heard both Beal and Quenton hurrying to their horses, hidden down in a draw. By the time he and Abigail had covered a few yards heading back toward No Consequence, Beal and Quenton flanked them like an honor guard. Ferguson caught up and rode behind so he could keep them all in his sights.

"What are you going to do with us, Ferguson?" called Slocum, not chancing a look back over his shoulder. If Abigail hadn't been prisoner, too, he would have tried to cut in front of either Beal or Quenton and stir things up a mite. If he got Ferguson firing at his own men, that might cause enough confusion to turn the tables. But Slocum dared not try anything like that. Abigail might be too slow to understand what was going on when six-shooters were leveled and men were ready to kill each other.

"Anything I like," the swindler said with a laugh. "It's going to be a real pleasure. In both your cases."

"You won't get away with this," Abigail said. "The town will be up in arms if you harm one hair on our heads. They'll come after you because we don't have any crime in No Consequence. My neighbors would never cotton to killing, and I assure you they'll never let you steal their money."

"We'll see about that. Now shut up. Both of you."

Slocum fumed as they rode slowly behind the buildings lining the town's main street. Adam Westfall stood on his soapbox in front of the small town hall and harangued a crowd into buying more bonds to insure that the railroad would actually reach No Consequence. From the infrequent glances Slocum was permitted between the buildings as they rode steadily, it seemed that Westfall had half the town's populace out at his rally, whipping them into a buying frenzy.

"He's damned good, isn't he?" asked Ferguson. "I never heard a man lie with such conviction."

"The only conviction you're likely to see is when the judge sentences you to jail!" raged Abigail.

"Now, how is it that such a pretty woman can be so downright dumb? If you'd thrown in with Westfall and the rest of us, you could have been rich, too."

Slocum saw they were heading toward the shed behind Abigail's store. The door stood open, and he got a good look inside. Someone had rooted through her inventory already, as if they knew she wasn't going to be in any position to complain. Slocum worried about that since it meant Ferguson and the others worked according to an established plan and that everything was going their way.

Steal goods from the stores for their getaway, steal the money from the bank—and they were free, rich men.

"Get in that shed. Beal, Quenton, see that they're tied up real tight. Especially Slocum. It wouldn't hurt me none if some blood flowed from his wrists."

"You do your own dirty work, Ferguson," complained Quenton. "Why even bother keeping them prisoner? Just put a couple bullets in them. I'll do it, if you want. I'm not squeamish."

"And you haven't been paying attention," Ferguson said caustically. "There'll be time for that later, but not yet."

Beal and Quenton stripped Slocum of his six-shooter

and knife and began lashing his hands securely behind his back, until the thin rawhide strips cut deeply into his flesh. The blood Ferguson had wanted trickled from the cuts. Slocum resigned himself to some additional pain in an hour or two. The blood would soak into the strips, dry and then the rawhide would start to contract.

While the men roughly bound Abigail, teasing and tormenting her and enjoying her futile protests, Slocum cocked an ear to catch Westfall's words booming throughout town. From the cheers at what he said, apparently the mayor had already collected more than the hundred thousand. The "extra" he wanted amounted to another twenty thousand dollars.

"What morning are the people of No Consequence going to wake up and find that you've held up their bank?" asked Slocum.

"Why hold it up?" asked Ferguson, laughing. "All we need to do is have Carleton open the safe. We can ride on out of town and nobody'll be the wiser for a long spell."

"You mean Carleton and Westfall will stick around and pretend they don't know anything about it?" asked Abigail.

"I don't give a rat's ass what those two do," said Ferguson. "Me and my boys will have the money. Let them try and take their share. Right, Beal? Quenton?"

Ferguson's two henchmen nodded reluctantly, as if they realized Ferguson might try double-crossing them, too.

"What about your other two partners?" asked Slocum. "Do they get a share, too?"

"What others?" demanded Beal.

"He's only trying to spook you," Ferguson said too quickly.

"You haven't told them about your partners from North Platte, have you? He's got two men camped out on the prairie. I'd wondered what you were going to do with them. Now I know."

"Shut up, Slocum."

"You're going to have them rob Beal and Quenton of their share. Where are you going to put their bodies, Ferguson? Beside Westfall and Carleton?"

"Shut *up*!" raged the swindler. He reared back, then swung with all his might. Slocum ducked at the last possible instant, but the barrel of Ferguson's rifle struck him a glancing blow that sent him staggering into the shed. Slocum stubbed his toe on a sack on the floor and went down in a heap, too dazed to stand.

"We'll take turns with your woman, Slocum. A dozen times each! Then we'll kill her and you. How do you like that?"

To get Beal and Quenton's goat, Slocum croaked out something about the men hiding out on the prairie, but the words were jumbled and too low to be heard. He grunted when a heavy, wriggling weight crashed onto top of him. Then they were plunged into darkness.

"John, are you all right? Let me get around."

Slocum felt the weight vanish from his back. Ferguson had shoved Abigail on top of him. The blonde sat heavily beside him and sputtered in her anger. By the time she was more coherent, Slocum had scooted around and propped himself up against a crate. The shed was as dark as midnight but slivers of light slanted in through poorly fitted wall slats.

"John, I'm so sorry. I never thought anyone would steal the money. What are we going to do?"

"Die," he said harshly, "unless we get out of here. I don't know why Ferguson didn't take Quenton's advice and kill us out of hand."

"Maybe he has something in mind for us?" Abigail sounded distraught and on the verge of tears.

"Is there any way he could frame us for robbing the

money?" Slocum leaned back and gathered his strength as he thought hard. Whether Ferguson tried to implicate them in the scheme mattered less than getting out of the shed. Slocum doubted it would be long until whatever Ferguson waited for happened and the time had arrived to kill his prisoners.

"I don't see how," Abigail said. "Everyone knows I'm honest."

"That and a nickel will get you a beer," Slocum said. "When the farmers find their money's all gone, they won't much recollect anything honest about you, if Westfall points the finger in your direction."

"Is that what they're going to do? Have Carleton remove the money, then blame it on us?"

"They're planning something else," Slocum said. "I just rode in, so they couldn't have factored me into their scheme." He said nothing about Abigail. She would make a perfect scapegoat if Carleton and Westfall remained after Ferguson rode off with the money. Two pillars of the community accusing the chief fund-raiser of fraud was about perfect. Ferguson might stick around and claim he had caught Abigail and Slocum trying to escape.

The money, of course, would never be found. Westfall could tell the townspeople Abigail had hidden it somewhere, perhaps out on the prairie. No amount of jail time or even outright torture would ever recover the money.

That sounded likely to Slocum, but he thought there had to be more. He saw no reason for Carleton and Westfall to stay in No Consequence to point fingers and dish out blame, even if it cleared their names.

Ferguson obviously sought to double-cross Westfall and Carleton as well as Beal and Quenton. The men who rode with Ferguson back in North Platte were out on the prairie somewhere and figured into the scheme. Since neither Beal nor Quenton knew about them, they had to be Ferguson's hole cards.

"My hands are getting cold, John. What are we going to do?"

Slocum forced himself around until he saw Abigail illuminated in a tiny sliver of light oozing around the shed door: Tears ran down her cheeks and glinted like morning dew drops.

"What's in the shed that we might use?" He sneezed at the flour dust hanging suspended in the tight enclosure. A bag or two had leaked and sent the fine powder into the air like a mist. Motes danced like fireflies in the patches of light sneaking into the shed.

"Nothing. Food, nothing else. I kept all the tools inside so they wouldn't rust." Abigail sniffed loudly. "As if the rain was bad this year. It's been a drought year. Never seen it this way."

"Abigail," Slocum said sharply, "did you leave a knife or scissors out here? Flailing around in the dark's not going to get us out of here, and the rawhide's too tough for me to break outright."

"I . . . I might be able to untie the knots if you wiggled around," she said.

Slocum tested the leather strips and knew that would be a waste of time. Even if her fingers didn't get slick with his blood, the knots were too tight. The strips had to be cut off.

"Are there any nails poking through the wall? I might use the point to scratch through the rawhide."

"The shed's built pretty well. The only reason there's any light coming in is because of the drought. The wood's shrunk."

Slocum rolled over in the tight quarters and got to one of the cracks so he could press his eye to it. The field of vision outside wasn't too great, but it was enough to convince him Ferguson hadn't left any guards.

"We might shout and draw attention," Abigail said when he told her.

"That won't work. Everyone's at the rally, forking over their last penny to buy more of Westfall's bonds." Slocum heard the mayor's voice urging everyone to take a risk on the future, to buy bonds that would insure the town's survival—and their own. Slocum almost believed him as he listened to the beguiling, honeyed words.

"Do you think you can kick open the door?" asked Abigail.

"That was a mighty strong lock you had on it," Slocum said, remembering the glint of the shiny steel padlock. "I might kick the door off its hinges." He rolled back, braced himself against a crate and shoved his feet against the door.

Gritting his teeth and grunting with exertion, Slocum pushed as hard as he could. Nails squealed as they slowly came out of wood, and he felt the door giving slightly, but he wasn't going to be able to kick open the locked door by himself.

Slocum gasped and sagged, defeated for the moment.

"Let me help, John. The two of us together might turn the trick."

"Is there a wall where it might be easier to kick out a panel or two?" he asked.

"The door," Abigail said firmly. "This is our best bet."

"I felt it give a little. Not much, but some. The nails holding the hinges might be ready to pop out."

"Both of us, together," she said. He felt her warm body settle next to his and wished they were in the shed under different circumstances. Slocum caught the woman's scent, felt the light touch of her blond hair on his face and experienced the heat from her sweating, straining body.

"There," she said. "I can get my feet next to yours."

"Not there," Slocum said. "Position them under so we can put all our weight against the hinges."

Abigail squirmed a bit more and then applied her full

strength with Slocum's. Almost immediately the hinges began pulling free of the wood and then a loud crack like a gunshot echoed through the shed as the door broke.

The door swung around on the hasp and lock and twisted at a crazy angle, letting in sunlight.

"We did it! We can get out!" cried Abigail, struggling to her feet. She recoiled as Slocum collided with her in his haste to escape, also.

Slocum fell face down and wiggled forward, only to stop when he saw a pair of dirty, scuffed boots blocking his path. He twisted around and looked up into the muzzle of a six-shooter.

"If Ferguson hadn't told me not to plug you, you'd be dead right now, Slocum," snarled Quenton. "Get back into the shed."

"Go on, shoot me," Slocum said, taking the only chance he could. A gunshot might bring the crowd, still cheering and crying out every time Adam Westfall told them of new riches to be brought to their town on the railroad.

"That's too easy," Quenton said. He reared back and kicked Slocum in the face.

Slocum tried to avoid the kick but was only partially successful. The toe of the boot crashed into the side of his head and knocked him out. By the time he struggled back to consciousness he thought he had gone completely blind.

Nowhere did he see the faint light of the sun filtering into the shed—and he was certain he had been put back there. The air was still filled with flour from torn sacks, and the crate against which he rested was as hard as before. Small, animal-like sobbing sounds alerted him to Abigail nearby.

"I think Quenton might have blinded me. I can't see anything," Slocum said, trying to get her mind off her own woes. "Can you help me?"

"Y-you're not blind, John. It's late. You've been unconscious for hours and hours."

"The sun's set already?" He shook his head and immediately regretted it. Things rattled around painfully inside.

"Yes," she said, sniffing hard and fighting to control her emotions. "Quenton and Beal nailed the door shut this time. They worked for an hour, cursing the entire time. There's no way we can hope to kick it open again."

"If they're standing guard outside, we wouldn't get too far anyway," he said, shifting into a sitting position.

"I heard them go hours ago. They were laughing and carrying on. I think Westfall's gotten all the money he can. Those horrible men might already have taken it from the bank."

"Any gunshots?" Slocum asked.

"What do you mean?"

"I didn't get the impression Ferguson was going to leave either Carleton or Westfall alive." Slocum frowned as he spoke. This didn't seem right. Ferguson was a swindler, not the kind of *bandido* who put on a mask, drew a six-gun and then robbed a bank. Slocum felt there were undercurrents in this con game he didn't understand.

"They're coming back!" Abigail cried.

"Maybe it's someone else," Slocum said. He shouted a few times, only to be rewarded with a slug ripping through the wall a few feet above his head.

"You shut up in there, Slocum." Rafe Ferguson sounded downright pleased with himself, in spite of his stern tone.

"What are you going to do now, Ferguson?"

"Me and my boys are riding out of No Consequence. Soon as you get out, you're free to do whatever you want to come after us."

Abigail let out a sigh of relief but Slocum tensed. Ferguson wasn't stupid. After all he had done to Slocum, he had to know he had made an implacable enemy who would track him to the ends of the earth.

The sloshing sounds and the smell of kerosene told Slocum that he was right.

"He's going to set fire to the shed!" Slocum warned Abigail.

Before the woman could answer, a loud snapping like a sheet ripping stopped her. The kerosene-drenched dry wood walls were encased in flames, and they were trapped inside.

14

Slocum coughed as the heavy smoke filled his lungs. His eyes watered, and he felt the heat from the fire beginning to blister his skin. Abigail was screaming, but her cries were muffled by the roar of the fire devouring the shed. Rolling over and getting to his feet, Slocum turned his head away from the worst of the flames, then let out a cry of his own as he charged like a bull.

He slammed hard into the wall and rebounded, stumbling and falling onto a crate. His foot caught on a bag of flour, and distant memories of other fires came to him.

"Get down," Slocum shouted. "Face down. There's going to be one hell of an explosion."

He began kicking at the bag until the toe of his boot worried open a gash. Then he twisted and sent flour into the air. The explosion as the small particles ignited blew him back—and through the shed wall.

For a moment he lay stunned on the ground. Then he realized he was staring up at the clouds of smoke trying to hide the nighttime sky. Stars twinkled and a distant moon poked above the buildings at the far end of town. Slocum sucked in fresh air and rolled over, getting back to his feet.

"Abigail!" he shouted. "Get out of there!"

No response. Slocum took a deep breath and charged back into the shed, kicking away burning wood blocking his way. The blonde lay in a heap next to the crate he had fallen onto. Abigail moaned and stirred.

"Come on. The roof's going to crash down any second." He prodded her with his boot, then turned and used his numbed fingers to find her earlobe. He caught the tender flesh between thumb and forefinger, then pinched down as hard as he could. Abigail screeched in pain, but it was enough to clear the fog in her brain.

"Out!" he repeated.

Slocum shielded her the best he could from the intense fire as they blundered back through the side of the shed and for some distance before collapsing in the dirt. Both of them panted harshly as the smoke cleared their lungs. Slocum's ears rang. Then he heard another clanging, and one not born inside his head.

"Fire alarm," Abigail said. "I hope they get here in time to save my store."

Slocum had a better view of the store and knew it was too late to save it. If the town's volunteer fire department responded quickly enough, they might save the rest of No Consequence. Otherwise, everything was going up in flames.

"Can you do anything to get free?" asked Slocum. "I don't see anything to use to cut my bonds."

"My hands feel like ice, John," she said. "I can't even flex my fingers."

"Over here!" Slocum shouted when the first of the firemen came staggering up. The man was half-dressed and carried a paltry bucket of water. Then others formed a line and began passing filled buckets to the man in front to throw on the fire, while youngsters took the empties and ran to the rear of the line to get them filled again.

Slocum's cries were heard by one of the boys, who

came over and stared at them with wide eyes.

"You all right?" he asked, peering nearsightedly at them. "Miz Stanley? Is that you?"

"Patrick," Abigail gasped out. "Do you have your penknife with you?"

"Shore do. Ever since you gave it to me, I never let it outta my sight."

"Use it!" Slocum snapped, turning so the boy could see the bloodstained rawhide strips around his wrists.

"What happened to you? Who hogtied you?"

"Cut the cords," Slocum said. The boy gulped, dug in his pocket and pulled out a small knife. He opened the blade and sawed through the tough leather until Slocum grunted with pain. The rawhide parted and circulation began again in his hands. He rubbed his wrists until he felt them tingle and sting. By then Patrick had freed Abigail.

"I better get on back to the fire line," the boy said, looking anxious. He wasn't sure why Abigail and Slocum had been trussed up, but he wasn't going to ask.

"Thank you," Abigail said.

"It was nuthin'," the boy said modestly. "Gave me a chance to use that knife you give me."

"That's about the finest gift I've ever made," Abigail told him, smiling. The boy rushed off, tucking his penknife back into his pocket.

"They're not going to save your store," Slocum said. The shed was a total loss and the fire had already jumped to the roof of the larger structure. Beams collapsed inward and set the store on a course of complete destruction.

"They'll stop the fire before it spreads much more. See?" Abigail pointed to the way the bucket brigade had split in two and threw water on the buildings on either side of the general store.

"That wipes you out, doesn't it?" asked Slocum.

"I'm afraid so." Then Abigail stiffened and resolve caused her jaw to set. "I'm ruined, but there's still the bond money to save. There's nothing I can do now but keep Carleton and Westfall from stealing the townspeople's money!"

She took off at a run. Slocum was slower to follow. He ached all over and knew he ought to get a doctor to smear some salve on the blisters and burns on his face and arms, but he shared Abigail's determination. She felt betrayed by men she had admired and thought to be her friends. Slocum had a score to settle with Rafe Ferguson and his gang, including the mayor and banker.

"Slocum! Lend us a hand. We got ourselves a real fire going here!"

Slocum didn't know who called out to him but he slowed and let Abigail go ahead.

"Don't know how this started but it looks like it was in Miss Abigail's shed." The man, already dark with soot, stopped and stared at Slocum. "You musta been right up close to the fire to get that scorched. You'd better let the doc fix you up."

"How much of the town can you save?" Slocum asked.

" 'Bout all of it. Might lose two or three more stores. The bookstore went up like a skyrocket. But the bakery and pharmacy are gettin' a soaking now and aren't in any danger."

"What about the bank?" Slocum asked.

"Naw, it's at the far end of town. No way this dinky little fire could reach it. Why, the one we had last year, took danged near all of main street. We—"

Slocum left the man reminiscing about prior fires and lit out after Abigail. He had to dodge through the part of the crowd not actively working to put out the fire. When he reached the boardwalk in front of the bank, he saw Abigail standing and staring at the plate glass window as if she were in a trance.

"Are you all right?" Slocum asked.

"I don't know what to do," Abigail said in a low voice.

Her face was dirty with soot and she sported more than a few burns and cuts of her own, but Slocum thought she was about the prettiest thing he had ever seen. The distress she felt over Carleton and the municipal bonds was obvious.

"Did you ask if anyone had seen Carleton or Westfall?"

"No one has, though I only asked a few of the women. Westfall disappeared after the bond rally and no one's seen him since, even in the saloon." The words were hardly out of the woman's mouth when an explosion knocked Slocum off his feet. He careened forward and crashed into Abigail, twisting hard as he took her in his arms to keep her from harm. His shoulders smashed into the bank's window, shattering it into a million pieces.

Half in the bank and the rest still on the boardwalk, Slocum shook off the fog that threatened to engulf him.

"What happened?" he asked.

"Let me help you, Slocum." Strong hands pulled him to his feet. "You all right, Miss Abigail?"

"I'm fine. Thank you," she said. "What was the explosion?"

Slocum wiped his eyes clear and saw the Prairie Delight Saloon engulfed in flames. His benefactor was one of the Gorman brothers—he couldn't remember which—who owned the saloon.

"Reckon a spark caught on my grain alcohol out back. No way of saving the old Prairie Delight now," Gorman said with resignation. "We'll be danged lucky if the whole town's not in ashes by morning." Gorman stepped back and looked into the bank, as if considering what was in the vault and how it might be removed for his own benefit. The expression changed to one of regret.

"You wiped out?" asked Slocum.

"Surely am. I can always help my brother Gus at the Corinthian Palace. It's far enough away so the fire won't reach it. Just damned bad luck that took my saloon. Excuse my French, Miss Abigail."

"I'm thinking the same thoughts, Paul," she told him. "My store is a total loss."

"We're wiped out together. Damned shame," Paul said, looking once more into the bank lobby.

Slocum decided it would be worthwhile having a witness for what he intended doing. He brushed the glass from his shirt, stepped into the bank and went to the rear, where the vault was partially hidden from the street.

The heavy steel door stood wide open.

Gorman pressed in behind Slocum. "Somebody cleaned out the bank!"

"Carleton," Slocum said, "and your mayor."

"What? How do you know it was them? Maybe Mr. Carleton saw the fire and took everything out so it would be safe."

"The vault would protect money better than anything else. I've seen banks reduced to rubble and the vault was intact, along with everything inside." Slocum walked up and, from the flickering light of the burning saloon across the street, saw that every penny had been taken.

"We got a passel of trouble, that's for sure. The fire purty near wipes out No Consequence and now the bank's been robbed."

"Go tell everyone," Slocum said. "I'll get on the robbers' trail."

"Mr. Carleton?" asked Paul Gorman, still skeptical. "You reckon you can find him?"

Slocum shrugged. Few men matched him when it came to tracking, but Carleton and Westfall might have several hours' head start. Rafe Ferguson and his gang would be easier to trail since they had stayed in town to set the fire and the tracks would be fresher.

At least, Slocum hoped so. With so many men hurrying about No Consequence, moving what they could to save it from the fire, bringing up water and trying to keep the entire town from burning to the ground, finding even Ferguson's tracks might be impossible. But Slocum had to try.

"I don't know what to do, John," Abigail said, tears rolling down her cheeks and leaving sooty tracks. "I feel so responsible for everything. The fire, the way Westfall and Carleton stole everyone's money—everything!"

He took her in his arms and held her while she sobbed. In a way, Slocum felt responsible, too. He'd had the gut feeling from the start that Ferguson was working a swindle, but he hadn't done enough to find out what it was or to stop it. Everything the crook touched became tainted. Slocum reached over to Carleton's desk and picked up the large bundle of bogus bonds sold at the afternoon rally but never delivered. It was as if Carleton—and Ferguson—had left them to taunt him. He started to crush them, then changed his mind and tucked the thick wad of worthless paper inside his shirt. But there was something missing, some part of Ferguson's scheme that Slocum still hadn't figured out.

That bothered him as much as their having nearly been barbecued behind Abigail's store.

"There's something else," Slocum said. "I just don't see what it is."

"What are you talking about, John?"

"Rafe Ferguson isn't a highwayman. He doesn't rob banks at gunpoint. He's too much a coward for that. He relies on swindling people. If he could make the same amount of money cheating that he could playing it square, he'd cheat every time. That's just the way he is."

"I don't understand," Abigail said.

"Rob the bank and set fire to the town to cover his tracks? That's not the way he works."

"Maybe Carleton and Westfall double-crossed him?"

"It would be the other way around. Ferguson has a couple men out on the prairie that Beal and Quenton didn't know about. Your two phony railroad directors will end up—" Slocum frowned. The scheme had fallen apart on Ferguson, and Slocum thought he knew how and why.

"We did it. Or rather, I did," Slocum decided. "I rushed things, and when you confronted them, they had to change their plan."

"What were they going to do?"

"They didn't plan to set fire to No Consequence. Ferguson did that to get rid of us and to cover the robbery. He probably hoped the bank would burn down and everyone would think the money was destroyed. But the way the scheme was supposed to work would have had everyone thinking nothing was wrong."

"I don't—" Abigail shook her head.

"The two phony railroad directors were supposed to show up in town. No matter what Westfall and Carleton told me, they were going to hand over the bond money to Beal and Quenton. The two would leave, meet up with Ferguson and then wait for Carleton and Westfall so they could divvy it up. Ferguson had some cockamamie story invented about how the directors had been killed on the road back to Omaha and the money stolen. Westfall and Carleton would be in the clear and the crooks could go their separate ways with their share, no one in No Consequence the wiser."

"I suppose it could have worked that way. But why would Carleton and Westfall stay in town if they had sucked all the money out of it?"

"Maybe they'd move on, but there wouldn't be wanted posters following them all over the West. And there wouldn't be angry farmers intent on tracking them down and stringing them up. Let a vigilance committee go after imaginary road agents responsible for killing the fake directors. They'd never find the culprits."

"Or if they caught someone, they'd string up the wrong men," Abigail said.

"Ferguson is never seen and never suspected of any wrongdoing."

"That might be why he intended to get rid of Beal and Quenton. Ferguson's partners, the ones you saw in North Platte, might do the dirty work and leave the directors' bodies for everyone to find. That would certainly make everything seem real."

"And we rushed them. They were afraid of you when you caught them red-handed discussing their plans," Slocum said, still chafing over how Abigail had barged in on the men. "They couldn't know if anyone else knew, so they decided to kill us and burn down the town to cover not only our murders but the bank robbery."

It all fit. But Slocum still felt he had missed something. Ferguson was a devious son of a bitch and a vindictive one. He and his two cronies might have been willing to kill Beal and Quenton to make the robbery look real, but also killing Westfall and Carleton would have alerted the town. The mayor and banker would have insisted on their cut of the loot before ever returning to No Consequence. Ferguson must have plotted something else to take care of those two.

Slocum shrugged it off. What Ferguson intended was less important than catching him before he vanished into the sea of grass that was Nebraska.

"I need to get on his trail right away," Slocum said. "If I don't catch him quick, there's almost no chance at all of finding him and the money."

"Hurry, John. I'll try to do what I can here, but the town's in such poor shape now. Many of the buildings are in ruins. All because of me." Abigail started sobbing again.

"You couldn't know your mayor and trusted banker

would turn into crooks. They might never have done anything wrong if Rafe Ferguson hadn't come along with his tempting scheme."

"Might be," Abigail said. "Go on. Do what you can, John."

She kissed him and then spun and left the bank lobby, her boots crushing the broken glass. Slocum followed, wondering where his roan had gotten off to. He didn't put it past Ferguson to have stolen the horse, but he was pleasantly surprised to see the stallion grazing at the far end of town, near the only saloon still standing.

Somehow the horse had gotten away from Ferguson and his cronies and had come here. Slocum opened the saddlebags and found his spare Colt Navy. It took a few minutes to load it and get it back on his hip, where it hung with reassuring pressure. He swung into the saddle and guided the horse in a wide circle around town, heading for a spot well away from the now charred shed.

The horse smelled the smoke and shied but made no effort to run toward Paul Gorman's still blazing Prairie Delight Saloon. Other buildings had either burned to the ground and were nothing but smoldering embers, or had been saved. The great fire was almost out.

Slocum tried to figure where Ferguson might have left and began a slow arc that would cross that part of the prairie. He hunted for hoofprints, for bent grass, for any sign that three riders—or perhaps five, if Carleton and Westfall were with Ferguson and the fake railroad directors—had passed by. The wan light of the quarter moon helped his search, but after three hours Slocum had to admit defeat.

He'd have to wait until dawn to continue, but by then the swindlers would have a twelve-hour head start on him.

Slocum stood in the stirrups and looked out over the grasslands. All he saw was restlessly moving vegetation, like the surface of an ocean. Where Ferguson and the others had gone might remain a mystery forever. With great reluctance, Slocum turned back toward town to find Abigail and let her know of his failure.

15

Slocum rode back into No Consequence, his eyes blurred and watering from the heavy, smoky pall hanging over the town. Here and there he saw bright orange embers persistently glowing, but a half dozen laughing youngsters ran around pissing on the coals to put them out. From the gloomy looks on the faces of their parents, the kids were the only ones having any fun.

Slocum had seen towns completely devastated by quick-spreading fires. The majority of the buildings in No Consequence remained standing, because of the dearth of wood on the prairie. Brick walls tottered and roofs had collapsed where the fire had burned through the wood beams used there, but mostly the town had escaped the firestorm that could have killed them all.

Seeing Gorman pawing through the ruins of the Prairie Delight, Slocum jumped down and stepped over the hot spots on the dirt floor to where the man examined shot glasses and beer steins.

"Finding anything worth salvaging?" Slocum asked.

"Only the glassware. All the booze burned up quick. The walls collapsed and destroyed most of the bar and other equipment, what the fire didn't already chew up and spit out."

"What'll you do now?" asked Slocum.

"My brother's bailed me out a couple times before when I went bust. I can work for him a year or two, then set out on my own, but with my bad luck . . ." Paul Gorman shook his head. "Might be I ought to find some other profession."

"Don't go into doctoring, if your luck's as bad as you say."

Gorman stared at Slocum for a second, then burst out laughing. "That's a good one, Slocum. You ought to work behind a bar. You've got a quick way with jokes. Folks coming in to drink want that sometimes."

"Other times they just want to get drunk and shoot up the place," Slocum said.

"And how," Gorman agreed. He dumped the last of his intact glasses into a crate and hefted it. "You lookin' for Miss Abigail?"

"You know where she is? With her store all burned up, I didn't know if she had a place to stay."

"She found a hunk of canvas and some stakes, along with a blanket or two that didn't get too charred in her store. Said she was gonna pitch a tent out on the prairie west of town. I reckon she wouldn't mind it none if you went lookin' for her." Gorman grunted as he lugged the heavy crate out into the street. He set it down for a moment, spit on his hands, then picked it up with an easy motion, balanced it on his shoulder and headed for his brother's saloon at the far end of town.

Slocum knocked a burning coal from his boot and went back into the street. He walked slowly past the bank. No one had taken notice of the robbery yet. Their concern over the rest of the town's damage was still too great, but they would notice when they went to get the money needed to rebuild. Slocum wondered if Ferguson had torched the town to cover the robbery or had done it to afford himself enough time to get away.

Or maybe he had done it out of spite.

There were still too many questions about Ferguson's plot Slocum did not understand.

He continued to the end of town and walked in the direction Gorman had said Abigail had taken. The stench of burned wood faded behind him, only faint traces clinging to his clothing. By the time Slocum spotted the tent pitched on the top of a low hill about a half mile outside town he could barely put one foot in front of the other. He and Abigail had been through too much that night.

He trudged up the hill and paused a few yards away from the tent.

"Abigail?" he called.

"John? John!" The blonde came out of the tent on hands and knees, then got to her feet and rushed to him. She threw her arms around him and hugged him tight. "I worried something had happened to you."

"What could happen after being tied up and damned near burned alive?"

Abigail laughed and cried at the same time. She buried her face in his chest and only slowly pushed back and looked up into his eyes. Her intense blue eyes fixed on his green ones. He bent and kissed her, gently at first and then with increasing passion. She returned the ardor and added some of her own until they were both greedily devouring each other's mouth.

"I hope something more'll happen," Abigail said, pushing away. Slocum didn't follow her when he saw what she was doing. As she turned, she had begun shedding clothing. Her blouse was the first to go, leaving her bare to the waist. He caught glimpses of her fine, firm breasts as she turned from him, then coyly looked back over her shoulder and batted her eyelashes.

The coppery rings around her nipples pulsed as her excitement rose. Slocum watched the rubbery buds grow harder, longer, ready for his lips to kiss and mouth to suckle. He stepped forward, but she held out her hand to stop him.

Silently, he let her continue her striptease. It excited him watching her unfasten her belt, holding her skirt and then beginning to sway to and fro to get it over her flaring hips. Inch by inch Abigail lowered her skirt, giving him tantalizing glimpses of paradise. Just under her belly poked up a tuft of silky blond fur. It vanished as Abigail turned from him and bent forward, her bare buttocks inviting Slocum to step up and do what he wanted.

Slocum dropped his gun belt and got out of his shirt. Then he unbuttoned his fly and let his raging organ out. The tensions mounting in his body knew no bounds. He had to possess her. Now.

"Go on, John," she said in a sex-husky voice. "Do it. Take me any way you want, but take me now!"

She moaned softly as he stepped up behind her and ran his hands over the satiny curves of her rump. The flesh trembled under his touch. He gripped a double handful of taut buttocks and squeezed down. Abigail moaned louder. When he ran his hand between those meaty half-moons all the way to the fleecy slit hidden between her legs, he thought Abigail was going to collapse with desire.

She wobbled, and he supported her with his other hand, running his arm around her waist. Tensing his arm a mite, he drew her back into the circle of his crotch.

"Oh, so hard!" she cried, feeling his throbbing manhood now. "I want it all. Now, John, give it to me."

He pulled her back even more, his thick, fleshy cylinder driving between the slabs of meat as he hunted for the target they both wanted him to hit. The topside of his stalk ran between her nether lips and sampled the moistness bubbling from her innards. Slocum had to use both hands now on the sultry blonde's waist to hold her. Abigail trembled and moaned and began swaying as her knees threatened to buckle from the intense sensations lancing through her.

With infinite care, Slocum drew back, dipped down just a little and then felt her pinkly scalloped lips part for him. The purpled knob of his manhood sank an inch into her seething interior. Slocum hesitated now, letting the heat wash through him from her aroused body.

"Ready?" he asked.

"Hard, John, do it hard. Take me like a stallion!"

He could hardly restrain himself. The feel of her buttocks pressing into his groin, her body trembling like a thoroughbred horse ready for the chase, the way her breasts dangled down as she bent forward, all of it aroused Slocum to the breaking point. He slammed full depth into her and thought he was going to lose control like a young lad experiencing such carnal delights for the first time.

Abigail began bucking like an unbroken mustang, shoving her haunches back into him as hard as she could and rotating about to stir his length deep within her. Slocum held on, relishing every moment of being buried within her smoldering insides. Powerful muscles clamped down on him and tried to milk him, but Slocum was immovable. All he could do was stand like a statue and let the pleasure echo throughout his body.

Reaching forward, he slid his hand over her heaving belly and upward to her dangling tits. Slocum caught one nipple between thumb and forefinger and began teasing it. This produced even more activity on the beautiful woman's part. Abigail tossed her blond locks and threw back her head, as if she was a coyote ready to howl.

Slocum knew the feeling. He wanted to howl and cavort about as he stroked over her breast, leaving the rock-hard nipple and taking the entire mound of soft warm flesh in his grip. As if he kneaded dough, he began squeezing and pressing his palm down hard into Abigail's bosom. With his other arm still circling her waist, he lifted her up.

This caused him to enter her at a new and excitingly different angle. Abigail was past coherent speech now, mewling and moaning and crying out in ecstasy as he stimulated her on several fronts at the same time.

Breast and belly. Buttock and buttery warm interior. He stroked with his hand and arm and increasingly painful erection. Slocum slid from her and then rammed back with breathtaking speed. The heat around his length built as he felt her strong inner muscles grip down firmly on him.

He started moving with slow, steady, powerful strokes that set off the woman's ultimate ecstasy. Slocum clung on, trying to get as much from her as he could. As Abigail's climax faded, he began pistoning faster and faster, letting her down enough so she could rest her palms on her knees for support. But every forward thrust was too powerful for her and drove the blonde to hands and knees.

Without missing a stroke, Slocum followed her down and kept pumping furiously until he was no longer able to contain himself. The heat within his loins exploded and raced outward. Slocum heard a cry of delight from a distance and then realized it was Abigail again cresting her summit.

Then he sank back on his heels, staring at her rounded white buttocks now gleaming like alabaster in the dawn light. Slocum might have seen a more beguiling, lovely woman, but he couldn't remember when or where right now.

Abigail pushed up to her knees and looked over her shoulder at him, grinning broadly.

"I brought blankets for us to use."

"It'd be a shame to let those fine new blankets go to waste," Slocum said. He got to his feet and thrust out his hand to help the naked woman get up. Her bare skin rubbed against his as they kissed and then slowly made their way to the tent to continue their lovemaking. It was almost noon before Slocum wasn't up to continuing.

He lay on his back, head sticking out of the tent so he could stare up at the cloudless blue Nebraska sky. In the distance swayed the short-grass prairie and behind him what remained of No Consequence gave a mute reminder of Ferguson's treachery. As sweet as it was spending a few hours so delightfully with Abigail, Slocum knew he had to get on Rafe Ferguson's trail. He didn't know what direction the man had taken, but there had to be a clue somewhere.

Ferguson couldn't run far enough fast enough to get away from John Slocum. Slocum owed the man for everything he had done to the citizens of No Consequence, to Abigail and probably to Big Ben London.

"I can't go on, John," Abigail said.

"I'm all tuckered out, too," Slocum said. "You've damned near worn me to a nubbin."

"No, not that," she said, swatting at him playfully. "I meant I can't start over in town."

"What are you going to do?"

"I don't know. Everything came crashing down around me when I found Carleton and Westfall were no-account thieves and had been using me to bilk so many good people. How can I face the farmers and those in town after I convinced them to invest their money?"

"Won't be easy," Slocum allowed, "but you've got to do it. There might not be anyone else in No Consequence willing to go to the ends of the earth to bring the crooks to justice."

"I certainly have a good reason."

"Revenge," Slocum said, thinking of all the reasons he had to track down Rafe Ferguson. The sight of Big Ben toppling from his horse rose but was quickly replaced by another vision even less appealing. Abigail had been the prime force in selling the bonds. The people who had been bilked out of their life savings might not take too kindly to her, even if she claimed to be an innocent victim.

"I feel insulted," Abigail said primly. "They duped me. I did something good for the town, and Carleton and the mayor lied to me. They were out to steal the money all along."

Slocum fell silent as he considered all that had happened.

Then he asked, "You know any special place Westfall or Carleton would feel safe?"

"Do you think they would take the money from the vault and hightail it there to divvy up with Ferguson? I don't know, John," she said, pursing her lips as she thought hard. "Westfall and Carleton weren't the type to go out onto the prairie much. When they did it was always for business reasons."

"Let's get into No Consequence and ask around. Somebody might know more about their haunts. I've found that men fall into a rut, doing the same thing over and over from habit."

"But Ferguson isn't one of them?" she asked. "You seem intent on Westfall and Carleton."

"They look to be the best way of getting to Rafe Ferguson," Slocum said. He had no idea where Ferguson might hide out. The prairie stretched endlessly for miles, rolling gently and not affording much in the way of a lair. Slocum figured Ferguson and his partners would head for some faraway spot and not stay around any longer than necessary. He also figured there wasn't any love lost between the crooks from No Consequence and Rafe Ferguson.

They wouldn't trust one another and that gave Slocum his only chance of finding them.

He and Abigail dressed, got the tent and blankets rolled up, and walked back into town. The light breeze off the grasslands had carried away much of the charred smell, but the amount of wood that had been burned showed Slocum how much work was ahead in rebuilding the town. The brick buildings were still standing, but many had damaged roofs. In other circumstances, the fire would have been serious but not fatal to the town. But with all the money stolen, Slocum wondered if No Consequence would end up a ghost town.

Then he saw how determined the citizens were as they cleared the debris and began repairs. Even the Prairie Delight Saloon had the look of a place rising from the ashes. Paul Gorman and his brother hauled soot and debris from the middle of the main room where the bar had been. Slocum waved cheerily to them as they passed and Paul called, "Come on back when I get open again."

"When'll that be?" asked Slocum.

Gorman shrugged, grinned and said, "My brother's loaned me a bottle or two. Come on over right now, and I'll give you one on the house!"

"I'll take a rain check," Slocum said, itching to be on Ferguson's trail.

"Everyone looks so happy," Abigail said in awe. "I thought they would be as disheartened as I am."

"As you were," Slocum said, hearing hope in her voice. "How long will it take to get the store open again?"

"I need to sift through the ruins and see what's left, but—" Abigail stopped and stared. At the far end of town a few people gathered. Then more came out from their labors, until most of the citizens lined the main street to stare at the spectacle.

Slocum frowned when he saw the wagons all decked out in parti-colored crepe and bearing signs announcing the arrival of the Platte & Central Plains Railroad.

"What the hell's this about?" Slocum asked.

"I don't know," Abigail said. "It looks like a parade, but I don't know any of those men."

Seated in the back of one long wagon were four confused looking men dressed in their Sunday best. They huddled together, and when they separated they weren't confused as much as they were angry. One jumped to the ground and looked around before calling loudly, "Where's the mayor?"

Slocum went to the man and blinked as sunlight caught on the headlight diamond the size of his thumbnail holding the man's cravat down. Although a mite dusty, the man wore clothing that cost enough to keep most folks in food and shelter for a year.

"The mayor's not here," Slocum said, wanting to draw the man out to see what this was about.

"Then I need to speak with Mr. Carleton." The man scowled when Slocum didn't respond and the crowd went silent. "The town banker. This *is* No Consequence?"

"It is, sir," Abigail said, pushing past Slocum. "I'm Abigail Stanley. Who might you be?"

"Crandall Reed Davis, president of the Platte and Central Plains Railroad."

Slocum didn't know whether to laugh or punch out the crook. Abigail put a hand on his arm to keep him from doing the latter.

"Uh, Mr. Davis, there isn't any such thing as the Platte and Central Plains. That was all a swindle thought up by Rafe Ferguson. Our mayor and banker were in on it, and I suspect you must be, too."

"I don't know what you're talking about. These gentlemen are three of my directors and we're here for the ceremony of collecting your bond money to finance the spur into No Consequence."

Slocum had a sinking feeling that he had just discovered the twist to Rafe Ferguson's swindle, and it wasn't a gentle tweak.

16

"Where's the money? I need to get my crew started on laying track," Davis said, puffing out his broad chest and hooking his thumbs under the armholes of his elegant red brocade vest. He looked around, scowling at the perplexed citizens of No Consequence. "Well? What's it going to be? I don't care if Carleton's off fishing, I need the money. I have expenses and a railroad to run."

"Why'd you come personally?" asked Slocum.

"For the money, man. Are you deaf?" Davis roared.

"With three other directors and all those others?" Slocum pointed to the confused people huddled in the two wagons trailing the one Davis had ridden into town.

"There was supposed to be a ceremony. Mayor Westfall asked for a show of support from the Platte and Central Plains and this is it. I'm here, he isn't."

"I was in Omaha and nobody'd ever heard of the Platte and Central Plains," Slocum said.

"You, sir, are wrong. Very wrong. Now, where is the company's money? The sooner we are given the money, the quicker the railroad can come to town."

"There isn't any money," Abigail said, seeing how her neighbors looked to her to be their spokesman. It wasn't a role she had sought but one she found thrust upon her by circumstance. "The mayor and bank president stole the money."

"A pity," Davis said sarcastically. "However, I want my company's money now. Any further . . . ceremony . . . would be a waste of my precious time. We need to lay the track before winter if we want this to be a terminus by next spring."

"Sir," Abigail said, raising her voice. "I just told you we don't have the money. It was stolen by the very men who made the deal with you."

"And I said it was a shame. However, the township of No Consequence owes the Platte and Central Plains Railroad one hundred thousand dollars. Today. Now. This very instant. Those were the conditions of the contract."

"You can't get blood out of a rock," Abigail said.

Slocum watched Davis's reaction and went cold inside. Rafe Ferguson was a genius at concocting swindles that would leave him out of the picture after he walked off with his booty. This was one of his best schemes, since it pitted the citizens of No Consequence against the railroad officers and no one mentioned Ferguson's part in stealing the money. It was almost as if he had never existed.

Slocum wasn't going to let him get away with this.

"You are wrong, Miss Stanley," Davis said. "We were promised the money. We have a legally binding contract signed by your mayor. If you don't have the money raised by a bond issue, then No Consequence must find the money somewhere else."

"There isn't any," Abigail said with growing desperation, "and you might as well tear up that contract."

"I will not. My duty to my company and its shareholders will not permit such action on my part. I could be held criminally liable if I did so with no good reason. Moreover, since I hold a valid contract insured by the land holdings of No Consequence, I will exercise foreclosure rights."

"Wait a minute," Slocum said. "You can't foreclose on the town because the mayor was a crook."

"I can and I will." Davis snapped his fingers and one of the mousy men in the second wagon hurried forward to hand him a sheaf of papers. Davis leafed through them and found one that satisfied him. "No Consequence owns all the land in a ten-mile radius from the town hall. That is—" He snapped his fingers again and the assistant spoke up right away.

"Three hundred fifteen square miles," the man said.

"This contract guarantees title transfer to the railroad of three hundred fifteen square miles of Nebraska countryside if you do not give us the agreed upon sum of money."

"That'd take in my farm," called a man from the back of the crowd.

"And everything in town," Abigail said. "You can't steal our land!"

"It's not theft," Davis said coldly. "It's business. The Platte and Central Plains is building a spur line here, either using bond money or the proceeds of selling land owned by the township. Which it is lies beyond my caring."

"But—" Abigail sputtered.

"No buts. We shall return in one week for the money, since that is the last day of the grace period afforded by your contract. If there is no money forthcoming then, we repossess the land."

Jeers and catcalls followed Davis and the wagonloads of railroad officials as they left town, heading back toward Omaha. Slocum watched them go, shaking his head.

"This can't be legal," he said. "Adam Westfall is a crook and knew he was committing fraud when he signed that contract. He was in cahoots with Ferguson and Carleton and planned to steal the bond money all along. It can't be legal."

"We need to know for sure, John. Ride with me to North Platte. I know a lawyer there who can tell us what to do."

"Davis might be a fraud, too, another of Ferguson's confederates." Slocum rested his hand on the ebony handle of his six-shooter, then moved away from the sidearm. As much as he hated to admit it, a lawyer was the town's best chance for a peaceable settlement.

"We need to know, John. Please."

Slocum agreed to escort Abigail to North Platte. They left within the hour after coming to an uneasy agreement with the rest of the citizens to allow Abigail to speak for them.

Slocum felt as if it had been a hundred years since he'd ridden into North Platte. The town looked no different, except that the beeves he and his trail crew had brought up from Texas were long gone. He heaved a deep sigh and almost considered continuing south to see if Leonard Larkin would take him back as top hand. Somehow, Slocum doubted it. As much as Larkin had liked him, the rancher must have found someone else to run his spread by now.

A shiver passed down his spine when Slocum realized Big Ben London should have taken that job rather than accompanying Abigail to No Consequence as a guard for her supply train. Instead of a decent job, Ben had earned himself a grave out on the prairie.

"There's his office. I've employed Mr. Bottoms several times for minor legal work, but I trust him enough to ask about this. After all, the fate of an entire town depends on his answer."

Slocum said nothing. He didn't trust lawyers since they were always looking at things from the corner of their eyes when they ought to be staring squarely at a problem. He was a direct man preferring direct methods. It made him powerful uneasy that lawyers never did things the easy way.

Only the legal way—or the way they could bend and corkscrew and contort the law to go their way. Slocum's experience with a carpetbagger judge trying to steal his family's property back in Calhoun, Georgia, had soured him on lawyers, judges and the law.

"I don't know what he can tell us that Davis hasn't already," Slocum said.

"We need to find how to counter Davis's arguments."

"He might be in cahoots with Ferguson. We should have found out before coming here." Slocum wasn't happy that he had not trailed Crandall Davis to see where he headed when he left No Consequence, but it had seemed more important to stay with Abigail then. The long, hard ride to North Platte had changed his mind. Davis had to be an accomplice in Ferguson's swindle and might even have rendezvoused with Westfall and the others, though what Ferguson gained by continuing the fraud this way, long past taking the money, was beyond Slocum.

He dismounted and held the door open for Abigail, who hurried into the lawyer's office. From the look of the room, Stan Bottoms did a good business, although no client was currently pouring out his troubles to the lawyer. A man with thinning sandy hair and pale gray eyes looked up from behind a large, well-polished cherry wood desk. Bottoms took off pince-nez glasses and laid them to one side as he rose.

"Miss Stanley, so good to see you again." Bottoms spoke affably enough but he kept his gaze fixed on Slocum, waiting for Abigail to introduce them. The lawyer looked uneasy when Abigail took the solitary chair and left Slocum standing, unintroduced.

"Mr. Bottoms, the entire town of No Consequence has a problem. A big problem."

"Maybe not," Slocum cut in. "What can you tell us about the Platte and Central Plains Railroad?"

Bottoms shook his head, then shrugged rounded shoulders. "Never heard of it, but that's not unusual. New companies spring up like toadstools after a good spring rain. Very few last as long as those toadstools, though."

"What about Crandall Reed Davis?"

Bottoms's eyebrows rose. This time he nodded, then leaned back in his chair and tented his fingers under his chin.

"I have heard of him. He is a principal partner in at least three railroads. If he claims to back this Platte and Central Plains line, rest assured that he does. He's a hard man but an honest one. Honest, that is, for a railroad magnate." Bottoms attempted a smile to go with his mild joke and saw how it failed.

"Oh, my," Abigail said, her hand covering her mouth.

"Please, Miss Stanley," Bottoms said, turning to a side table and taking a pitcher and drinking glass. He filled the tumbler with water and handed it to Abigail. "What is the problem?"

Slocum listened as Abigail rushed through the entire sordid affair.

"So the money has vanished along with the banker and mayor?" Bottoms pursed his lips but Slocum saw a hardness coming to the man's watery eyes.

"That's right. What can we do?" asked Abigail.

"Nothing, I am afraid, unless you want Davis to place a lien against all property owned by the town and then go to a federal court for an order to seize it."

"But Westfall made the deal knowing he was going to steal the money!" protested Abigail.

"That doesn't matter. Adam Westfall was the legal representative for the township. Anything he did in that capacity is legitimate. Later theft is irrelevant."

"Davis can't seize the land like that. There are farms and—"

"Miss Stanley, he can. This comes under the rather odd legalistic term of 'anti-donation clause' and applies in full force. Look at it from the railroad's viewpoint. They were promised money, contract signed and legal, and they didn't get a dime of their due. If you were in their position, you would do whatever was necessary—and legal—to collect."

"There's no point bringing a spur line to No Consequence if the railroad has driven out all the citizens," Slocum said.

Bottoms shrugged. "That's something to discuss with Davis. I admit that I am at a loss to understand why running a line from Omaha to No Consequence is worth his notice. However, the farmland sounds fertile and valuable. Perhaps Davis intends to seize it, then resell it to recoup his losses."

"He hasn't lost anything!" cried Abigail, jumping to her feet. "He hasn't even started laying track yet."

"That's not the way the railroad or its stockholders would see it, Miss Stanley. If you want me to represent you, I might renegotiate a slightly better deal, but frankly, I don't think Davis is amenable."

"There's no way out of this?"

Bottoms shook his head.

In shock, Abigail left the lawyer's office. The hot Nebraska sun beat down on her as they stood in the street.

"I don't believe it, John. What are we going to do? I have to tell my friends and neighbors that they're going to lose their businesses and farms because they sit on land leased them by the town."

"If Bottoms is right, the law is on Davis's side. Will the people in No Consequence fight?"

"You mean take up arms and shoot at Davis? I don't

know," Abigail said, distraught. "I don't know what to tell them. But I have to go back. It would be easy to simply walk away, but I'm responsible."

"You didn't know Carleton was a crook," Slocum said, pleased that Abigail wasn't the kind to turn and run from trouble. It would have been easier for her to leave the townspeople to their problems since she had nothing else to draw her back. Her store was ruined and the land under it was Davis's property. But rolling over and playing dead wasn't in Slocum's makeup, and he was glad to see it wasn't in Abigail's, either.

"We've got a powerful lot of prairie to cover. Let's ride," Slocum said.

Abigail looked like a forlorn waif in the front of the meeting hall. She had told them as simply as possible what the lawyer had said about the anti-donation clause and the trouble the entire township faced. It hadn't set well with anyone, and Slocum didn't much blame them.

"I ain't gonna give them my farm. I'm leasin' the land from the town, not some railroad millionaire who wants to steal it away."

"Does this mean our bonds are worthless?" asked another man, clearly confused. "And that I'll lose my pharmacy, too?"

The roar that went up surpassed Abigail's ability to quiet them. Slocum stood, drew his six-shooter and fired once into the ceiling. The loud report caused such a sudden silence that the tumble of falling plaster could be heard in the back of the now silent room.

"That's better," Slocum said. "Miss Stanley's in the same boat as you. Don't go poking more holes in the bottom. Anyone have an idea to offer worth more than a bucket of rat spit?"

"We sent a letter to the sheriff over in Seneca but nobody's heard back from him yet," one man said.

"That's a start," Slocum said. "We need to do more ourselves. Does anyone know of a place where Carleton or Westfall might hole up around here?"

Before anyone answered, the town hall doors banged open and a well-built and even better dressed man strutted in. He carried a briefcase in one hand and a walking stick with a gold knob in the other.

"I'm glad I found you all together," the man said without preamble. "I represent the Platte and Central Plains Railroad and its stockholders."

"You a lawyer?" asked Paul Gorman, squinting at the newcomer.

"I have the privilege of representing Mr. Davis and his company," the lawyer said. "In such capacity, I have applied for a federal court order seizing all property within ten miles of this town hall. Further, I have requested a company of cavalry soldiers to enforce the eviction order."

"Aren't you jumping the gun, mister?" asked Slocum. "Davis gave the town another three days to get the money." Slocum wished now he hadn't wasted four days going to North Platte to find out how tight the legal noose around their collective necks was.

"Consider this a friendly admonition," the lawyer said, tapping his walking stick against the floor in imitation of a telegraph key sending a dire warning. "No opposition to this order will be tolerated, should any of you be foolish enough to consider gunplay."

The lawyer looked around the room, saw the stunned faces and smiled slightly. With that, he swung around and left, twirling the walking stick like a drum major's baton.

"Looks like the railroad's coming to No Consequence, whether you want it or not," Slocum said.

Pandemonium broke loose in the meeting hall, but Slocum didn't stick around to hear what they had to say. He slipped out into the cooling night breeze and looked around, trying to decide where he ought to start his hunt for Ferguson, Carleton, Westfall and the money they had stolen.

17

Slocum climbed wearily onto his roan and let the horse have its head. The stallion walked aimlessly, going first in one direction and then in another. The night had turned cool, for which Slocum was grateful. The daytime heat had been oppressive and had kept him from thinking clearly—or at least he wanted to tell himself that.

As the horse meandered across the prairie, Slocum kept an eye peeled for any tracks that might have been left by riders recently leaving No Consequence. He had wasted almost a week escorting Abigail to North Platte to talk to the lawyer, but he did not regret the time spent with her. She had talked of this and that and had convinced Slocum she was worthy of his help. Even if he hadn't intended to keep after Ferguson for killing Big Ben London, Slocum would have insisted on helping Abigail after hearing of her travails getting the general store started and how she had done so much to help her neighbors.

Slocum had thought they were lucky when the boy, Patrick, had found them and had a penknife in his pocket. Abigail had given it to him for doing minor chores around her store. It had been worth far more than the boy's work, but she had seen how he coveted the knife and had almost given it to him. Almost. She waited until Patrick had worked enough to believe he had earned the knife and had gained a sense of what his time was worth.

Abigail Stanley had done that more than once, with more than the children in town. Seeing a well-intentioned, honorable woman put into the position she was in now by swindlers made Slocum's blood boil.

He owed Rafe Ferguson and his gang more than the law was ever likely to mete out to them.

"That way," Slocum said, using his knees to turn his horse slightly so it headed due north. As Abigail had talked, Slocum had listened hard for any clue where the banker and the crooked mayor might have gone. The pretty blond woman told of the hardships endured by the settlers around No Consequence a year or two back and of the current crop of woes before Adam Westfall ruined their town so completely.

She had mentioned an abandoned trading post built by the American Fur Company years back as a way station for the Oregon Trail. An easier route to the south through Scotts Bluff had been scouted and the post fell into ruin. Slocum wasn't an expert, but he thought Westfall and Carleton were likely to hole up somewhere nearby where they thought they were safe. They would both know of the old fort and not expect anyone else to think of it.

Slocum hoped Abigail was right about its location. He rode through the silent night, only soft wind rustling the knee-high grass along the way. Forest sounds appealed to him more, but a certain serenity to the prairie soothed him right now. But as he rode he saw dirt cut up by shod horses and increasing amounts of grass pulled out in large clumps, as if hungry horses had grazed.

Dropping to the ground, Slocum studied what he had seen from the saddle and estimated at least five horses had spent some time nipping at the grass. A slow smile came to his lips. Five horses: Beal, Quenton, Carleton, Westfall and Rafe Ferguson.

Tracking in the night was hard, but Slocum saw they were traveling more or less in a straight line toward the spot where Abigail had said the abandoned trading post still stood. As he rode, Slocum checked his Colt Navy to be sure all six chambers were loaded and that he had a couple spare cylinders ready for quick swapping. Then he filled the magazine of his Winchester. He expected a hard fight and didn't want to run out of ammo before he got to Rafe Ferguson.

As the sky lit with pale pinks and gray turned to blue, Slocum came upon the trading post. It had been built like a Mexican mission, with thick walls in a square. The western side had bricks tumbling from it but would still hold back a small attacking army. But Slocum saw that the gates in the south wall had been ripped from their hinges and afforded an easy entry into the courtyard.

Slocum watched the post for more than twenty minutes, trying to determine how many men were camped inside. A small curl of greasy black smoke rose as he watched. Buffalo chip fire. The faint acrid odor reached his nostrils but gave no hint how many men cooked their breakfast over the guttering flames.

He dismounted and tethered his stallion to a clump of yucca, then advanced cautiously. Someone was inside, and he thought it was Ferguson and his gang. But Slocum didn't want to get caught between those inside and any of Ferguson's men who might be out prowling the prairie.

Reaching the south wall, Slocum pressed his back against the cool brick and felt some of the mortar crack and tumble noisily to the ground. He froze until it became apparent no one had heard the small sound, then he chanced a quick look around the doorway into the middle of the post courtyard.

Two horses were tethered at the back.

Slocum sucked in his breath and held it for a moment. Two? What had happened to the other three men? He came to a quick decision. Take out the owlhoots he could and worry about the rest later.

With a quick move, Slocum whirled around the gateway and leveled his rifle, just in case any of Ferguson's men were be waiting for him. The place seemed deserted save for the horses and the small fire sending its smoke up a chimney at the side of the trading post.

"Where's the bacon? I got the fire hot enough," came a loud call.

"How the hell should I know? You packed the victuals."

"Did not," came the querulous reply.

Slocum recognized Beal and Quenton right away. From the direction of the cooking fire and their voices, they had camped out in one of the kitchens on the west side of the trading post. Moving on cat's feet, Slocum went to a window and peered inside. Sitting at a table were the two men, tin cups filled with steaming coffee in front of them. The fire in the fireplace produced the smoke Slocum had seen. Dangling from a hook over the low fire was a dutch oven, and sizzling on the lid was a single slice of bacon. From the heady mix of odors, Slocum couldn't tell what else the pair cooked for breakfast.

"Want to play a hand of poker?" asked Beal, reaching for his side pocket.

"Hold it," Quenton said, pushing back from the table and going for a small pistol. The two weren't on the best of terms.

"Don't get so nervy," Beal said, pulling out the deck of cards and throwing them on the table.

"I got every right to after what Ferguson did to us."

"He didn't do anything. This is all part of the plan."

"Sure it is," Quenton said sarcastically. "You get kicked

in the head by your horse? Ferguson's never going to meet us."

"We've got—" Beal's eyes widened, and Slocum knew he had been seen.

Slocum took in everything in a single glance. He had been so intent on the men he had not seen the cracked mirror on the wall behind Quenton. Beal had spotted his reflection in it and was going for his six-gun.

"Slocum!" cried Quenton, also going for his six-shooter.

Without hesitation, Slocum fired his Winchester at Quenton but missed because he rushed the shot and was already swinging around for a shot at Beal. The two men scrambled and upended the heavy table to use as a shield. Slocum fired several rounds into the table, but the thick wood absorbed the bullets.

"How'd you find us, you son of a bitch?" shouted Quenton.

Slocum didn't answer. He knew the trick. Quenton would try to keep him occupied while Beal went for the killing shot. Slocum ducked back, looked up and saw that the trading post had once had a walkway around the wall where defenders held off the Indians. A ladder missing a few rungs leaned against the walkway.

Backing away, Slocum went to the ladder and made his way up. He had gotten halfway to the top when he saw Beal poke his head up through a hole in the kitchen roof. Both men fired simultaneously. Slocum was a better marksman.

Beal tumbled back down into the kitchen. Slocum knew the man was dead by Quenton's reaction. A deep-throated roar was followed quickly by a bull's charge out into the courtyard. Quenton had two six-shooters, one in each hand, and he blazed away wildly. Lead chipped at brick all around Slocum, but Quenton's anger kept him from drawing a good bead.

Slocum swung around and tried to get his rifle lined up, but his awkward position prevented it. He dropped his Winchester and then jumped, landing hard and rolling. As he came to his feet, he had his Colt out and ready to shoot.

Quenton was gone.

"I don't want to kill you," Slocum called, not sure he was telling the truth. Quenton might have been the man who pulled the trigger and killed Big Ben London. If not, he was still guilty of a powerful lot of crimes against No Consequence and John Slocum.

"You killed Beal. You killed my partner!"

"Did Rafe Ferguson desert you? He won't split the loot with you."

"He already did," Quenton called. "Damned fool didn't get hardly anything from that hick town."

"The banker cleaned out the vault. I reckon he and Rafe Ferguson rode out of No Consequence with at least a hundred fifty thousand dollars. Did you get your cut, Quenton?"

"You're a liar, Slocum. He didn't get anywhere near that much."

Slocum's harsh laughter infuriated Quenton and flushed him. The outlaw came rushing from where he had taken cover, both six-shooters firing. Slocum took aim and squeezed off one round that caught Quenton in the middle of the chest. The phony railroad director straightened and then collapsed bonelessly to the ground, both six-guns clutched in his fists.

Wary of a trick, but feeling in his gut he had made a good shot, Slocum approached the body sprawled in the dirt. He kicked one six-gun away and pried the other from Quenton's lifeless fingers. The lone shot Slocum had taken had gone right through Quenton's foul heart, killing him instantly.

Slocum searched the man and found only a few hundred dollars in scrip. He went into the trading post kitchen and found Beal dangling over the edge of the upturned table. Another quick search dislodged another hundred dollars in greenbacks.

"You sorry fools," Slocum said without rancor. Quenton and Beal had paid for their crimes. He stared at the pitiful handful of paper money taken from their corpses and knew it wouldn't make a dent in what the town of No Consequence owed the railroad. Slocum went back and searched the bodies again for any hint as to Ferguson's whereabouts.

He was sure that if he found Rafe Ferguson, he would locate the bulk of the money. The bodies yielded nothing. He turned to the men's saddlebags and found small scraps of paper among Beal's possessions. Slocum held up the paper and painstakingly made out the faded ink and the date. The hotel receipt had gotten wet, which had partially destroyed it, but Slocum was heartened by the date.

Beal and Quenton had to have ridden straight to the Omaha hotel from setting fire to No Consequence. He tucked the scrap into his shirt pocket, along with the scrip. It wasn't much of a clue, but it was better than nothing.

18

Omaha had gotten hotter and dustier since Slocum had been here a couple weeks earlier. But he reflected on how much had happened in that short time. He rode slowly past the rail yards and then his curiosity got the better of him when he saw a line of flatbed freight cars being loaded with steel rails and wooden ties. The men cursed and shouted and toiled in the hot sun as if they were slaves, never stopping for fear of offending their masters.

"Where's all this heading?" Slocum asked the foreman. The man was stripped to the waist and sheened with sweat on his leathery skin. He wiped his forehead as he looked up at Slocum.

"You lookin' for a job? We still need a gandy dancer or two. If you can swing a hammer and lay rail, we pay top dollar."

"Who signs the checks?" asked Slocum, but in his heart he thought he knew the answer.

"Mr. Davis, of course. You'd be swingin' steel for the Central Kansas and Nebraska road."

"Not the Platte and Central Plains?"

The man wiped away more sweat and laughed. "You could call 'er that, too. Mr. Davis, he thinks up more names for his lines than you can shake a stick at. This one's been under wraps for a spell but now we're movin'. Good to get this miserable lot of slackers off their collective asses and back to work. They been havin' it too easy in Omaha."

"Got the right-of-way problem taken care of out near No Consequence?" asked Slocum.

The foreman shrugged, obviously uninformed about such things. "You want a job or you just wantin' to waste the time of men who have 'em already?"

"Much obliged for your time," Slocum said, snapping the reins and moving on. Nowhere else in the sprawling rail yards were men working to get rails ready for transport. Speaking with the foreman had confirmed what he'd feared was true. Crandall Reed Davis was a legitimate railroad owner and the spur line was going through No Consequence, whether the town paid for it or lost all their surrounding land in the process.

Slocum looked around for Will Mason but the man had moved on. He wished him well and hoped Mason had a decent job again that'd keep him in fine Kentucky bourbon. Slocum fumbled in his pocket and drew forth the receipt he had taken from Beal. Holding it in the bright sunlight gave him a name and an address. He rode from the railyards and hunted up and down cobblestone streets lined with hissing gas lamps. A new trolley car rattled and clanked past to let him know how far removed he was from the sleepy, dusty town of No Consequence. After an hour of searching, Slocum found the address.

He drew rein in front of the Excelsior Hotel and let out a low whistle. Slocum was used to flophouses or possibly hotels where he didn't have to arm wrestle the bedbugs more than half the night. The Excelsior was a first-class establishment.

"Who says crime doesn't pay?" he muttered as he jumped to the ground and led his horse to a watering trough in the shade at the side of the hotel. He brushed off dust from the trail and then gave up when every whack brought forth new clouds of brown Nebraska prairie. It would take more than a few pats to get clean enough to be presentable in a place like this.

Slocum went into the lobby and drew immediate attention from several bellhops and the well-dressed clerk behind the registration desk. The people in the parlor looked askance at him, but Slocum walked steadily to the desk.

"I'm sorry, sir, we have no vacancy," the clerk said before Slocum got out a word.

"Not looking for a room," Slocum said, to the man's immediate relief. "I want information about one of your former guests. Maybe several."

"I'm sorry, we do not give out names." The clerk peered down his nose at Slocum and started to gesture to the bellmen to throw Slocum out.

"It sounds like you're sorry about a lot of things," Slocum said, "but you'll be sorriest of all if you want to start a ruckus." He stepped back a half pace and made a show of taking the leather thong off the hammer on his six-shooter. The worn leather, the hard-used Colt Navy and Slocum's cold green eyes caused the clerk to swallow hard.

"I'm sor—I mean, what can I do for you?"

"Sir. That's 'what can you do for you, sir.' "

"Yes, sir. Of course, sir."

"Two gents stayed here several days back named Beal and Quenton." Slocum pulled the receipt out and made a show of studying it. "Beal was in Room 223."

"Why, uh, yes, sir, that's true. I remember him. He claimed to be a railroad director."

"Claimed?"

"I know all those gentlemen," the clerk said haughtily. "He neither acted nor dressed like one. The other one—

Quenton, you said—said very little. He had the adjoining room."

"What about the other three men with them?"

"Others?" The clerk got a shifty expression that changed to pure greed when Slocum pulled out the wad of greenbacks he had taken from Beal and Quenton. The clerk never noticed the bloodstains on the money as he made a quick swipe that hid the bills from sight.

"The others," Slocum said.

"Ah, yes, I remember them, sir. A banker and a politician."

"And the other one who went by the name of Ferguson."

"Yes," the clerk said, as if he had bitten into a tart persimmon. "They held their meeting over there at the large table in the parlor. They parted on amiable enough terms but . . ."

"But what?" prodded Slocum.

"There appeared to be some suspicion among them. They were friendly but not friends."

"Where'd they go? Or are they still here?"

"Oh, no, no, sir, not at all. But there was somewhat more bonhomie among the three after the two directors departed."

"Where did they go? Ferguson and the other two?" Slocum rested his hand on the ebony butt of his six-gun to reinforce his question and to insure an honest answer. The clerk had already been bribed, but Slocum didn't think he had the look of an honest crook—he wouldn't stay bought.

"I am sorry but I don't know. That's the truth, sir! I think I heard them mention something about a campsite out on the Platte, but I might have been mistaken."

"When did they leave?" Slocum asked, a sinking feeling in his gut. He had come so close, but if Ferguson and the other swindlers had almost a week's head start on him, there was no way of tracking them down.

"Why, you missed them by only a few hours."

Slocum perked up at this. "Anything else you can tell me? Where along the Platte?"

"Waterloo? I don't know why that town sticks in my mind. Perhaps I happened to overhear it and didn't know I had. Sorry, sir, but—" The clerk talked to empty air. Once more his lobby was returned to its usual sedate, pristine condition.

The Platte River flowed to the west of Omaha. This time of year it was down a considerable amount but still a force to be reckoned with. The town mentioned by the clerk was more of a dock than a town, providing some barges for moving freight up and down the river when it was fuller with spring rains.

Slocum doubted he would find anything worth mentioning in Waterloo, but it gave him a place to cross to the other side. Rafe Ferguson and his gang had returned to Omaha for some reason and then had gone their separate ways. Where Ferguson headed now was a mystery, but one Slocum would solve. He doubted the swindler intended to go back through North Platte or anywhere near No Consequence, but crossing the river meant Ferguson had some destination to the west in mind.

Or the south. Slocum heard the mournful whistle blow on a freight train heading down toward Kansas and wondered if Rafe Ferguson might not be going into Texas eventually. While he couldn't rightly remember, Slocum thought he had heard that Ferguson had family down around San Antonio.

The trip across the river went quickly on the small ferry, and Slocum soon found himself riding southward, wondering if he were on a wild goose chase—until he spotted three men riding along the flat bank of the river not a mile ahead. Slocum sucked in his breath and held it, worrying that they weren't the trio he sought.

Then he began to worry that they were Ferguson and his partners. Not much grew along the flat banks of the river to hide him should any of the men look back, and tackling the three of them would prove more than he could handle alone. Slocum slowed the pace and let the hot sun hammer him and his horse all afternoon long. When twilight came, he picked up the pace, although it was scarcely cooler. By the time he spotted the campfire, he knew he had found his quarry.

Ferguson sang boisterously, not caring if anyone overheard. Slocum would have recognized that voice anywhere.

"We done it, we really done it, boss," spoke one man. Slocum moved closer to watch them. When they unrolled their blankets and drifted off to sleep, he would strike. He could get the drop on them and escort them back to Omaha and the law.

Slocum touched the wad of worthless bonds he had taken from Carleton's bank and knew Ferguson and his cronies had a lot to answer for.

"I can't believe Westfall was so dumb," Ferguson bragged. "We'll have the money tomorrow morning and be on our way south."

"I can't wait to get to Fort Worth," the other gunman said. "I got me a filly there who'll help me spend all that money. How much was it, Ferguson?"

"Almost a hundred thousand dollars," Rafe Ferguson said. Slocum heard the change in the man's voice. The other two didn't. "Why don't you go on down to the river and get us some more water. This coffee's too strong and I want to dilute it."

"Coffee's fine," the man said. Then he saw the way Ferguson glared at him. Grumbling, he grabbed a pot and started for the Platte River gurgling loudly some fifty yards distant, leaving Ferguson with the other man. The way the man hobbled a little on his way to the river told Slocum this was the one he had winged before the North Platte saloon.

Slocum had intended to get the drop on them together, but this gave him a better chance. He slipped away and hurried after the man intent on getting water from the river.

As Slocum came up behind him, his Colt Navy drawn and ready to make the challenge, a shot rang out back at the camp. Startled, the man with the pot half-stood, turned and lost his balance when his gimpy leg failed him. His feet shot out from under him on the slippery mud and he fell heavily. The dull crunch as he hit his head on a river rock wasn't as loud as a gunshot but it was certainly as deadly.

Slocum hurried to the man and checked. He was as dead as surely as a chicken when a farmer wrings its neck. Searching the man's pockets yielded nothing. Then Slocum faded into the night when he heard footsteps rapidly approaching.

"Jase!" Ferguson called. "Jase! Something terrible's happened. Your brother's dead." Ferguson stopped and stared at the silent, dark body, then lifted the six-shooter he had carried hidden at his side and looked around.

"Who's out there? Did you kill him?"

Slocum moved like a ghost through the night, returning to Ferguson's camp. Sprawled on the ground, a bullet in the center of his back, lay Jase's unfortunate brother. Ferguson had sent one man to the river so he could back-shoot the other. Then he stalked Jase, intending to finish him off. The two brothers wouldn't be around to divvy up the loot from No Consequence.

Slocum had been wrong about Rafe Ferguson. The man *was* a murderer as well as a swindler. Or had the lure of so much money been too great? Ferguson had lied to his partners about the amount stolen from the bank. Beal and Quenton thought it was only a few hundred dollars—and they had been content. Slocum wasn't sure if Ferguson had sent them on their way with vague promises of rendezvousing later, or if they had lit out for territory they knew.

However it was, they were dead by Slocum's hand.

Slocum wondered what had happened to Westfall and Carleton. From what he had witnessed so far, he doubted they had fared any better than Ferguson's other partners.

A quick search of the camp, however, failed to unearth the stolen money.

"Slocum. I might have known," came Rafe Ferguson's cold words.

Slocum spun and fired at the same instant Ferguson did. A hammer blow struck Slocum in the chest and knocked him back, but he didn't feel the hot slug rip through his chest as he expected. He looked down and saw a burned hole in his shirt and an outward paper explosion from the bonds he had shoved inside. The thick wad of bogus bonds had stopped the bullet.

But Rafe Ferguson didn't have any such luck. Slocum's bullet had caught him squarely in the right shoulder. The man had turned and started to run, only to trip over his partner's dead body. He clumsily tried to stand but by then it was too late.

Slocum towered over him, Colt Navy cocked and pointed at the back of his head.

"I ought to blow your stinking head off," Slocum said. "Give me a reason not to."

"The money!" cried Ferguson. "I'll split the money with you. There's almost one hundred fifty thousand dollars! You ever see that much in your whole life, Slocum? It's yours. Don't kill me! I'll give it all to you!"

"Where is it?"

"Those fools from that hick town went along with

everything I said. It was too easy swindling them. I told them we had to hide the money for a spell until nobody was looking for it any longer. We . . . we buried it. Real close to here, on our way from No Consequence to Omaha."

"So you and your two partners—the two you just double-crossed—were going to dig it up and keep on riding," Slocum said.

"I didn't kill Jase. He—You killed him, Slocum. You're as much a murderer as I am!"

Slocum's finger trembled on the trigger. If it hadn't been for the money, he would have ended Rafe Ferguson's foul life then and there.

"Where'd you bury it?"

"Jase and Pete, they didn't pay a whole lot of attention. We're almost sitting on it. I told them we had another couple miles to go. We can dig it up, you and me, Slocum, just us!"

"Show me."

Slocum stepped back as Ferguson rolled over. The man's shirt and coat were soaked in blood from the profusely bleeding wound. Ferguson was so excited he hardly noticed, but Slocum didn't want him dying—yet.

"Let me patch you up," he said. "Any tricks and you'll be with your partners in the Happy Hunting Ground."

Slocum stripped Ferguson's jacket back but left it around his waist, the man's arms trapped in the sleeves. He tore away part of the shirt and used strips from it to bandage the wound. Slocum had shot up something important inside Ferguson from the way it refused to stop bleeding, but a little pressure finally let the bullet hole crust over.

"Damn, Slocum, I'm light-headed," Ferguson complained. From the way he wobbled and walked, Slocum doubted the swindler was faking. "But I know where the loot's buried. That tree yonder? See it? It's a sweet gum, just like down home."

Together they went to the large tree. Ferguson sat down, before he fell over, and pointed to a pair of protruding roots. The dirt between them had been freshly turned.

"There it is. What a sweet haul it was, too. All ours, Slocum. Yours and mine. Go on, dig it up so we can count it."

Slocum watched Ferguson out of the corner of his eye, but the man grew lethargic from lack of blood. A few quick scoops cleared away the dirt covering a large money bag.

"Yeah, there, that's it. Rich," Ferguson said, revitalized by the sight of the money bag.

Slocum opened it, peered inside, then upended it to dump out strips of newspaper. He started to accuse Ferguson of further treachery, but the look on the swindler's face told Slocum that it was the crook who had been double-crossed.

19

Slocum kept looking over at Rafe Ferguson to be sure he didn't fall off his horse. The man was as pale as a ghost and wobbled whenever he tried to lift his head to see where they were going. The bullet wound oozed constantly, and nothing Slocum did stopped it. Ferguson needed a doctor to get the bullet out of his shoulder and to sew up whatever was ripped up inside.

"Double-crosser, damn mayor, damn him," muttered Ferguson.

Slocum would have laughed at Rafe Ferguson if the man hadn't been so close to death. The swindler had been swindled good and proper by a couple men he had considered hayseeds. How Carleton and Westfall had substituted the cut paper for the money hardly mattered. They had let Ferguson set the rules and then they had used them to their own advantage.

"Where's Westfall now?" Slocum asked. "Is Carleton with him?"

"They weren't friends. Hated each other. Worked together for the money. But they musta been friends enough to switch the money on me like they did." Ferguson began rambling. Slocum found a man with a barge willing to take them across the Platte, and they were quickly on the road leading to Omaha. Slocum hoped Ferguson lasted long enough to tell the law what he had done.

A slow smile came to Slocum's lips as he reached down and touched the thick wad of bonds still inside his shirt. Ferguson's bullet had lodged in the bonds, proving they weren't as worthless as everyone claimed. They had proved invaluable by saving his life. Then the smile faded. Abigail's troubles—and those of everyone else in No Consequence—didn't go away because he had caught Rafe Ferguson and seen the other four into their graves.

The real crooks were still scot-free and had the town's money.

"I need to find the marshal's office," Slocum called to a man standing on a corner waiting for one of Omaha's trolleys to come by.

"Police station's down the street two blocks, turn left and keep going till you see it," the man said, looking sickly at the sight of the blood caking Ferguson's shirt.

"Much obliged," Slocum said. By now Ferguson was delirious and ranting. They rode for another ten minutes before they found the police station. Slocum dismounted, helped Ferguson down and half-dragged the man up the broad granite steps into the posh station.

"Don't you go bleedin' on me clean floor, bucko!" shouted a police sergeant from behind a desk. He surged around and caught up Ferguson as the man sagged.

"No luxury car for me. Not like that bastard wanted. None now," Ferguson said and then he passed out.

"What's he about now, boyo?" asked the sergeant. Three other blue-uniformed officers joined him.

It took Slocum the better part of an hour to explain what had happened and Rafe Ferguson's role in it. He left out the part about gunning down Beal and Quenton. Their bodies were far beyond the jurisdiction of the Omaha police. For all that, Jase and Pete had died outside it, too, but the sergeant sent word to the sheriff, and Slocum spent another twenty minutes explaining everything.

The sheriff was more interested in the murders committed by Rafe Ferguson than the Omaha police, and that suited Slocum just fine. But the law, both local and county, refused to hunt for Westfall or Carleton, having their hands full with Ferguson and the crimes Slocum had charged him with.

By the time he stepped back into the bright Nebraska sun, Slocum was hungry and exhausted. He considered finding a restaurant for a big dinner or a saloon to buy something liquid and hard enough to wet his whistle but what Ferguson had said kept rolling over and over in his brain, like a scrap of paper caught in a dust devil.

Luxury car. Ferguson said there wasn't going to be any luxury car for him, Slocum mused. He mounted and rode for the railyard. Darkness had fallen and the freight train loaded with rails and ties to build the Platte & Central Plains—or whatever Davis decided to finally call the spur line to No Consequence—was long gone. Dozens of other steam engines puffed and clanked around the yards.

Carefully picking his way through the jungle of steel rails, Slocum eventually found a siding where a dozen fancy parlor cars were lined up. The men who owned the companies used these cars, men like Crandall Davis.

Maybe even men like Carleton and Westfall.

The first half dozen of the cars were pushed back to the ends of their sidings and were dark. One was in the middle of extensive renovation, the gold leaf on the fixtures inside not thick enough for the car's owner. But one car was brightly lit, and from the look of the three ladies of the night making their way up the back steps and going inside, it was also occupied.

Slocum dismounted and walked to the car. Standing on a box allowed him to look inside. His hand went to the six-shooter at his hip, then he relaxed. Lounging on a fainting couch was Adam Westfall, two of the soiled doves ministering to him. Across the car the banker Ed Carleton worked on the intricate fastenings of another whore's bodice. From the way his fingers fumbled and missed easy ties, he had been drinking heavily.

Slocum stepped back and looked at the layout of the car. The party went on in the back half. The front section was dark and apparently off-limits to the ladies of the evening. The Cyprians might not be allowed into the sleeping quarters, but Slocum felt no such constraint. He went to the far end of the car and climbed the steps. The door was securely locked, as he had thought it would be.

Going around the side of the car showed the windows were similarly fastened. Slocum went to the door again, but this time looked to the awning above the platform. He jumped, caught the edge and pulled himself up to the roof. Any noise he might make would certainly be drowned out by the excited squeals from the women.

It took him only a few seconds to locate the ceiling hatch, also locked. But this lock broke easily as he clubbed it with the butt of his Colt. Slocum opened the hatch and dropped into the closed section of the parlor car. Two rather spartan beds were placed on either side under the windows, allowing an aisle down the middle of the car.

Letting his eyes follow the narrow aisle brought him to a safe, but Slocum had the feeling he wouldn't find anything there. If any thief broke in, he would go immediately to the small locked box and probably wrestle it outside where it could be dynamited.

It was too easily removed for Carleton to use it.

Slocum began rummaging under cushions and the mattresses and hit the mother lode under one large overstuffed sofa beside the safe. The cushions crinkled strangely. Carefully pulling one open brought forth a cascade of greenbacks.

Emptying the cushion and stacking the money, Slocum continued his hunt and found another cushion similarly crammed with scrip. Only when he finished did he replace the money with the bogus bonds he had carried with him from No Consequence. Somehow, the bullet through the center of the worthless paper seemed more fitting an omen for the two thieves than having their loot taken.

Using a pillowcase from one bed to hold the money, Slocum went to the locked door connecting the two sections of the parlor car. A peephole allowed him to see what was going on.

Both Westfall and Carleton were still enjoying the favors of the ladies they had chosen for the night.

Slocum retreated, going back through the ceiling hatch. He made certain it was closed behind him before he dropped to the ground, cinders grating loudly under his boots. Neither Carleton nor Westfall was in any condition to care about strange sounds outside their little section of paradise.

The pillowcase with its valuable load slung over his shoulder, Slocum went back to his roan and mounted. He rode slowly through the rail yard until he found the stationmaster, asleep in his quarters. It took fifteen minutes to figure out Carleton and Westfall intended to move their fancy parlor car onto a train heading for New York City. It took another fifteen minutes of dickering and a few hundred dollars from the pillowcase before the stationmaster agreed to hold up their departure for a day or two.

Only then did Slocum ride out to find a telegraph station and send a priority message to Abigail in No Consequence detailing where the swindlers might be found. She could swear out legal warrants with the sheriff in Seneca, and he might ride over himself or have the Omaha sheriff arrest them. Whatever happened, Carleton and Westfall weren't going anywhere for a day or two—and they weren't taking the money they had swindled with them.

Feeling good, Slocum headed for No Consequence and Abigail Stanley, the money securely stuffed into his saddlebags. He didn't want to miss the celebration when he turned it over to her.